Love Story With Birds

Derek Furr

Fomite

Burlington VT

ISBN-13: 978-1-959984-66-5
Library of Congress Control Number: 2024945142

Fomite
58 Peru Street
Burlington, VT 05401
www.fomitepress.com

08/28/2024

The Definition of Melody—is—

That Definition is none—

—Emily Dickinson

Contents

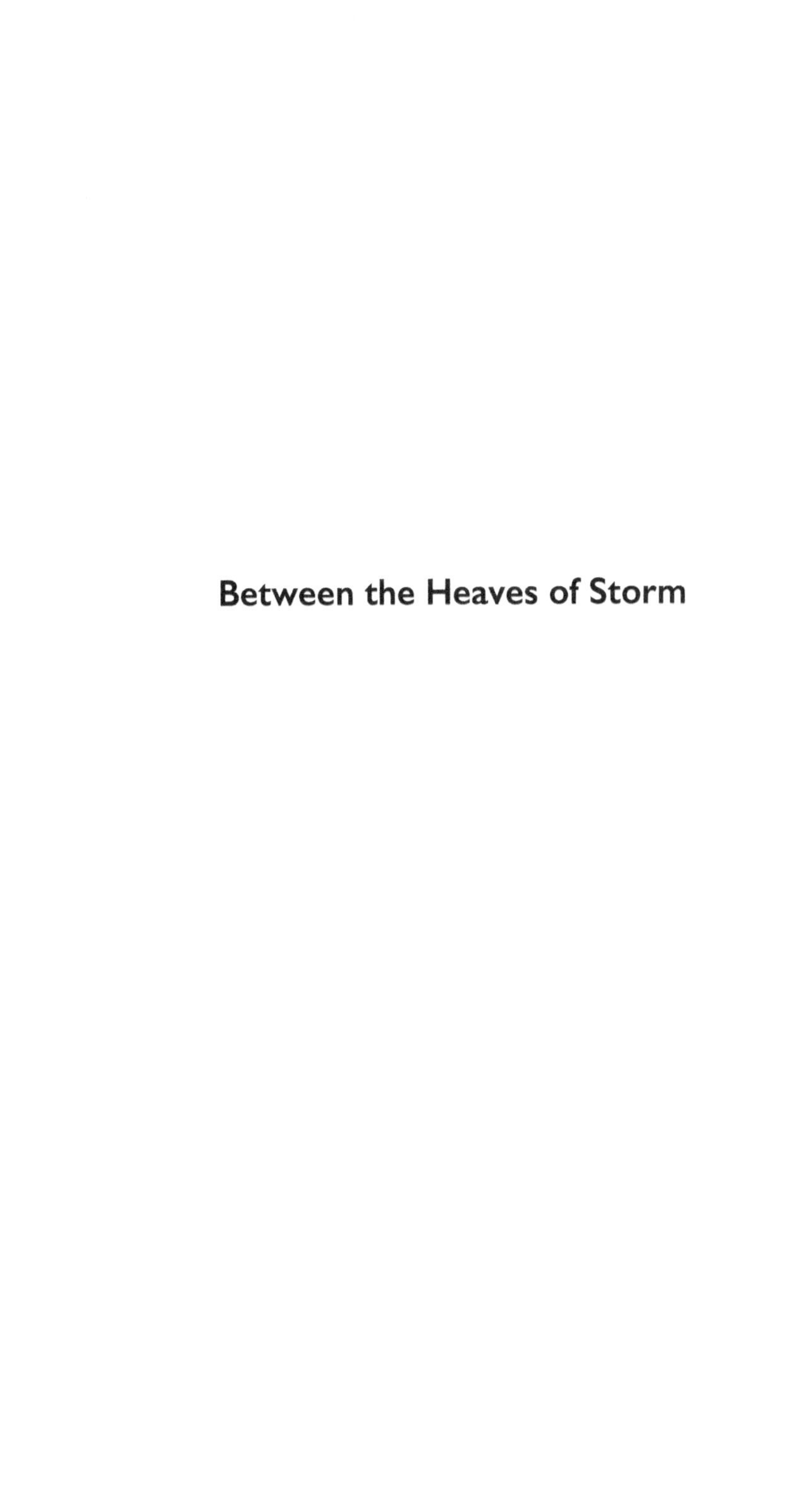

Between the Heaves of Storm

Addiction

She floated along the aisle to pass the peace, angling off to a window during the hymn. Talk of debt seemed to wake her, and threat of the soup kitchen's closure sharpened her focus. She declared that someone should step up to prevent all this loss.

"Had the first trip bored me, or scared me," she would explain at meetings, "I might have been a pediatrician or a pastor." But recovery eluded her like a toddler, giggling. Her next days were photocopies until the paper bin emptied.

"How to proceed?" she wondered, finding herself in a woods, the voices having silenced. Leaves covered the trails, snow would soon follow, and who among the passersby could be trusted? Meanwhile, a barred owl stirred in the beeches above, preparing for night.

Seattle Non Sequitur

(Waiting for the Link, January 2020)

Wet night
Smear of moonlight
Far above the city.

Fog freezes to the platform.
Mastiff and master shuffle
Near the edge.

Among Hennessey empties
A rat walks the rails
Filmed by every teenager's phone.

What should the theme music be?
One expects sax, or blues guitar.
Solo, wordless.

But it's a pipa, amplified,
Played by a woman in wool
Under her pink umbrella.

A bearded man declares
The singularity is coming.
His companion offers him gum.

No train arrives on time,
People scroll their feeds,
The damp seeps through gloves

And clings to eyelashes.
"I need a gun," says the beard.
"I need a fucking gun."

Sacred Heart

Judy volunteered at Sacred Heart Second Hand Thrift Shop. She sorted and laundered donations in the back room every day and took home what she needed. She always asked before she took anything, but no one objected, because her kids and grandkids--eight of them packed in their two bedrooms—had to be kept in clothes. That's what the thrift shop was meant for, Judy said, not for the likes of Sparrow.

Judy watched Sparrow drift around the dress rack with her skinny legs and bare midriff, like a teenager even though she had to be at least twenty-five. How was it fair that Sparrow took the thrift shop discount? She had no kids. She paid no rent because she lived in her grandmother's spare room or with her latest boyfriend. She could work if she cared to lift a finger, since it's no problem for a pretty girl to get a job at a cash register. Instead she strolled into Sacred Heart Second Hand for a skirt or scarf or at least nylons two or three times per week. Judy had counted as many as four times in a recent week, and there is just no way she needed all those clothes for herself and her grandmother. The old Episcopal ladies were sweet but gullible, even worse when someone was pretty like Sparrow, because everyone knows that she's reselling half of what she takes home.

Judy was sure of it. She knew every blouse, skirt, and pair of shoes that came through the shop, and she had seen them walking around on girls who never darkened the doors of the Sacred Heart. How do you explain that except Sparrow buys them on discount then turns around and sells them to the college kids at one of those vintage clothing markets?

"Vintage clothing." If Judy had only known about that racket, she could have made a fortune from the polyester dresses that she let mildew in her dead mother's trailer house. Think of what people will pay for faux jeweled necklaces and brooches! There was a table of them at the corner of the park that was always mobbed with willowy blonde girls. Judy stopped once out of curiosity. There was a tiger's eye bracelet. She could keep the kids in pork chops for a week for what that guy was asking for it. He seemed shady. His arms were hairless, and he smiled when he spoke.

The bracelet was heavier than she expected. Maybe the stones were real. What if one of those college girls had offered to buy it for her? She wasn't proud, but never mind. Her wrist was too thick anyway.

Sparrow left Sacred Heart with a bag of scarves. It burned Judy up.

Sparrow's grandmother was nearly blind from diabetes.

She pulled her chair within inches of the TV and turned it up loud, as if she were deaf, too. Every time Sparrow came home, she had to remind her, "Grandma you're not deaf just blind!" and turned it down, otherwise you couldn't hear yourself think. Not that Sparrow was cruel about it. She kissed her forehead and made her a peanut butter and banana sandwich. That, and fruit cocktail cups, were all her grandmother would eat.

Sparrow went to her bedroom and draped the scarves on Olivia's arm. Currently Olivia wore a cute yellow A-line that needed the right accent. It was daffodil, not mustard or honey, so several of the scarves were too subdued. The pink sheer with the stripes—that ensemble would be noticed. She pulled the shade to get the best light then snapped and posted a photo to her site, Olivia Oldstyle. Her phone pinged 16 times within the first minute, and within five, she had two DMs asking the price.

Sparrow was putting away as much money as she could before her court date next month. The public defender would try to plea her out of serving time for that outburst with the tequila bottle, but she had said frankly the chances were slim. The dependent grandmother helped, and if Sparrow could show the capacity for a payment plan to cover the plaintiff's medical bills, the prosecution might agree to rehab and community service. After all, the plaintiff had started the fight and crushed her friend

Kat's hand before Sparrow intervened. It was self-defense, arguably. And the plaintiff's tox screen was colorful, whereas hers was just alcohol. So there were mitigating circumstances. But the plaintiff's jaw was broken, and she might lose an eye. Besides, Sparrow had a record, and she had mouthed off at the cop.

Sparrow received another direct message, this time from an Emma who would give $50 in cash. She lived in the toney housing development at the edge of the bus line. It was a hike, but Sparrow could deliver in person and save the shipping cost. She would be back in time to feed her grandmother her supper sandwich and fruit cup.

Judy missed the bus, so she would be late getting home from the thrift shop. Elaina would not be pleased.

Judy's daughter and her twin toddlers had moved in with Judy four months ago when Elaina's boyfriend Hector began hitting her again. Judy warned her that he was no good, but Elaina had to see for herself. So it goes. Elaina arrived in the middle of the night with both kids screaming. Her nose was bleeding and her left eye swollen shut. Hector tried coming for her the next day, but Judy made sure he knew that was a mistake. She called her oldest son. Mike wasn't good for much but he was pro-tective. He said text me when that bastard shows up, so she did, and while Hector was outside Judy's apartment window, drunk and swearing about how those twins were as much his as hers, and how he'd drag all of them home by the hair of their heads, Mike and his friends rolled up carrying baseball bats. There was cursing, followed by sounds that reminded Judy of when they tossed laundry bags onto the loading dock at the thrift shop. She didn't watch.

Elaina was 17 and could have made something of herself if she had stayed away from boys. That's what Judy had told her, and here she was, dropped out of high school one year from finishing. She was artistic. She had designed and painted the sets for the school musical, the one with the singing cowboys. She made As in history, the subject that had ended Judy's school career at grade ten. But Elaina liked the rowdy guys, and when she started being seen with Hector, Judy tried to talk sense into her. Oh well.

Judy did appreciate having Elaina around to help with Mike's three cast-offs, who were preschool age and home all day. They were good kids but wouldn't watch TV for very long, so someone had to keep an eye on them. Elaina hated being home with five children while Judy was at Sacred Heart. But beggars can't be choosers, and what choice did they have? Judy's other two sons were tomcats, in and out of the house at all hours, usually home just long enough to eat the leftovers and make piles of dirty clothes for Judy to deal with. She assumed that they were going to school often enough to pass. They had a knack

for picking up odd jobs, it seemed, because they sometimes left cash in the loose change jar that Judy kept on
the refrigerator.

When Judy got home, Elaina was flushed and shaking
all over, the way she used to get as a child when she had
a tantrum. It was all she could do to manage the twins,
she screamed, who were still not off the breast and never
would nap. She couldn't keep up with Mike's kids, too,
always into the cabinets or sneaking into the yard, thank
god it's fenced, and complaining about being hungry but
never eating anything but goldfish and chocolate milk.
What was Mike doing besides drugs? Why couldn't he or
their mother lend a hand? She knew that Judy was doing
her best, she wasn't blaming her, but if she had to spend
another day like this, she would pull a Sylvia Plath.

Judy wasn't sure who Sylvia was but she got the idea.
It was no use making awful threats like that, she said. Did
she want to ruin Judy's life more than it already was? Elaina
and the grandbabies were the most important things in
the world to her, and Elaina shouldn't talk that way. If the
twins would learn to take a bottle, Elaina could go to the
thrift shop, and Judy would stay home with all the kids.

Elaina collapsed sobbing in a kitchen chair with the
twins pulling at her skirt and crying. She should go lie
down, Judy said. Judy would settle the twins and then
make tea. Mike would probably take his kids back if she

asked him to, but their mother was no good, and Judy worried about what went on in that apartment. They weren't Elaina's responsibility, though, so Judy would come up with a solution.

On the bus back from her delivery, Sparrow wondered why the Emmas she sold to were always so sociable. This one had chatted with her for fifteen minutes about spaniels and bellybutton piercing. Sparrow enjoyed it, which bothered her, because Emmas lived in a fantasyland. Not that she begrudged their privileges, just found their myopia annoying. If one of them asked her to move in, of course she would do so without giving it any thought. Some Emma or some Bradley could say come be my wife, and she wouldn't even bother to go home and pack, except for her grandmother. If it fell apart in a couple of months, would she be any worse off?

Today's Emma modeled the ensemble for her right there in the paved driveway. This happened often, too. Sometimes it was like they wanted to make sure it fit, and she had to remind them that there were no returns. But today's Emma was the other sort: eager to be photographed and posted as a happy customer. She was so pleased that she gave Sparrow an extra five bucks for the bus.

Sparrow's friend Opal was flopped on a beanbag chair next to Sparrow's grandmother when she got home. Opal hadn't exited her Goth phase, so there was never anything in Sparrow's line to suit her, but she supported the business venture. She followed Sparrow to her bedroom and said hello to Olivia. "Girl, you're stark naked," she said and tied a scarf around her neck. She listened to Sparrow describe today's Emma and concluded that Sparrow should charge more. "If you have to market to those types, make them pay."

"She wasn't so bad. Like I told you, they usually aren't."

"Don't be fooled. It's Emmas that wind up in the prosecutor's office."

"Sure. But if one of them offered to pay your rent, you wouldn't refuse."

"Of course not. Take from the rich. But I wouldn't believe that they actually cared."

"Who said this was about caring or not caring? All I mean is that most Emmas I've dealt with are good customers."

"You mean they pay well, and I say that they would pay more."

"That's not at all what I'm talking about. They like my ensembles, they go on about them and tell their friends. They have little conversations with me, about the clothes, about other random stuff. It's kind of nice."

Opal put a belt around Olivia's waist. "And what I'm saying is it's fine to want their approval of your business, but it's a slippery slope if you need them to approve of you."

A week later, Elaina and Sparrow met. While Judy was at Sacred Heart, Elaina scrolled the vintage clothing pages to distract herself from the misery of childcare. Elaina adored the checkerboard dress on Olivia Oldstyle and messaged the site that she'd pay cash. Sparrow replied that she would be right over.

Elaina's skin tingled. The tomcats had put $25 in the can this morning after her mother left. She would use it, and her mother would never know the difference. They'd just stocked up on groceries, so it's not like anyone was going to starve. She was not about to feel guilty for this impulse buy. Even now Mike's kids were fighting and would wake up the twins, who had finally gone down for a nap, and if there weren't some joy in her life soon, she would pull a Sylvia for certain.

When the doorbell buzzed, Elaina suddenly worried about how the owner of Olivia Oldstyle would react to their little orphanage in the hood. She was obviously an Emma. Why would an Emma even come out here? She opened the door to a girl with weaves and distressed nylons. She could have lived next door. Elaina was startled, but so relieved that she asked Sparrow in. She apologized for the noise and diaper smell and offered to make Sparrow tea.

"Tea?"

"Is that weird? I'm sorry, that's weird. You're probably in a hurry."

"Not really, I just don't get offered tea very often."

Mike's three had gone silent since Sparrow entered. They hovered around Elaina and kept their eyes on the stranger. Elaina gave them goldfish in bowls of chocolate milk and told them to watch TV while she gave the lady tea. They did as she asked, and she was quick to whisper to Sparrow that a miracle had occurred. Now could she try on the dress?

Elaina still had a bulge from the pregnancy. She wanted to lose it, but who could exercise? Sparrow started to remind her of the no-returns policy, but stopped when she saw Elaina's eyes well up. There she was in her bra and panties, holding up the checkerboard dress as if it were dropped from heaven. Whether it fit wouldn't matter. It was a bit tight in the bust since Elaina was nursing, but it was flattering through the hips, and Elaina had nice legs. Did she want to pose for a happy customer shot?

Elaina felt a fool for how emotional all of this made her. The twins were still asleep, the cast-offs were watching TV like normal children, and even though she'd never be able to wear this dress in front of her mother, she would have it when things were better. It was going to seem desperate, but she asked Sparrow to come by again.

Elaina was an expert with nails and could give a manicure or pedicure or both, if that was an enticement.

Sparrow became a regular for tea with Elaina while Judy was at the Sacred Heart. Elaina didn't speak of it with her mother, because her mother sympathized with her in suffering, but would have no respect for her joy.

Soon there was a change at Sacred Heart. Patricia, cashier on Tuesdays and Thursdays and the oldest volunteer, passed peacefully in her sleep, and the Episcopal women asked Judy to watch the register as her replacement. Judy confessed that math was not her strong suit, but she knew how to handle money and make change, and she would be honored. They would need her for the full six hours on those days, and since this was asking a lot of her, they invited her to take two families' worth of groceries from the Community Pantry each week, as well as whatever she might require in clothing for the children.

All the way home Judy fretted about how Elaina would react. Two days per week, she would have to watch the kids for six hours at a stretch. But double the groceries could not be passed up. And Elaina should think about her mother for a change. She wouldn't be on her feet. She would be in the front, representing the shop. It was an honor.

"An honor? Why don't they pay you?"

"No one gets paid at the thrift shop, not in money at least."

"None of the other volunteers need to be paid. You're poor. They should pay you."

"Don't talk like that. We're not poor. You make us sound like trash."

"Not poor? Mother, we take clothes and food from a church charity. We use SNAP. We have two bedrooms for eight people. I'm just stating a fact."

"We do fine."

"If we're so fine, why do you need to get double the pantry items? I'd honestly rather go hungry. I'd rather go hungry than have to spend even more hours alone with a house full of children that nobody wants."

"Elaina, shut your mouth. I love my grandchildren, and you love them, too. You're being hateful."

"And you're being selfish. Don't think I don't know what this is all about. This 'honor.' It makes you feel like somebody."

"What are you talking about?"

"They're just using you. A bunch of rich old lady do-gooders who ought to be paying you at least minimum wage, for God's sake, but you do it for fuck-all-nothing because you feel honored. Of course, you get even more hours away from this dreary same shit, different day, orphanage, so who am I to blame you?"

"This is what you really think, Elaina?"

None of this argument was any use, Elaina thought. Every child in the house was bawling at the top of its lungs. She had to find a way to get out on her own with the twins.

Now Judy was embarrassed to think of the cashier position as an honor, but it was almost the best thing to happen to her in such a long time! The only thing better was having Elaina home again, which was a constant struggle, yes, but worth it to her. Mike and Elaina hadn't turned out perfect, but she must have done something right because they came to her when things fell apart or were more than they could handle. She hadn't had that— no spouse, no parents. She was on her own, unlike Elaina, who ought to take a moment and be grateful for what she has.

Elaina had never told Sparrow that her mother volunteered at a thrift shop. The bartering for food and clothes was too embarrassing to acknowledge. But the next day, she was so exhausted and angry with the impending threat of extra childcare that she unloaded on Sparrow about her mother's new "job." As Elaina stirred sugar into their tea and circled back for the third time to having been "abandoned by her mother," Sparrow couldn't temper her feelings any longer.

"It's only a few extra hours. And she'll be bringing home more money, right."

"Sure. But the hours feel like days."

"Where is the place she works?"

"It's just a box store. I don't really know."

"Couldn't you work there instead? I mean, once you can stop being a milk machine?"

"Probably. Why are you taking her side?"

"Because you're getting something too, right? She's letting you live and eat here, and most of the week she's home to help you out. I'm not seeing how that's selfish of her."

"You don't know how she can be. So self-righteous."

"I still don't think that you get to complain too much if you're benefiting from her."

Elaina stopped herself from responding. She stirred her tea. She walked over to the bedroom door and checked on the twins.

"I'm just saying if you're miserable, you should leave. It would be hard, but maybe it wouldn't be worse."

The twins were sleeping. The cast-offs had gone quiet as if they sensed the tension. Elaina looked around at her misery. Sparrow didn't understand yet, but she might eventually, if Elaina didn't bore her to death or scare her off. She imagined Sparrow getting up to leave and not coming back.

Her skin became clammy, and her heart raced. The past few weeks had been so much better with Sparrow coming around, and she was about to drive her off with her complaints. Elaina felt dizzy, as if she was going to fall over, but she couldn't let that happen. No doubt Sparrow would never come back if she keeled over like some Victorian housewife.

When Elaina's knees buckled, Sparrow leapt up and caught her. She was heavier than Sparrow might have imagined, and they both ended up on the floor. But it was a soft landing. Elaina was panting. For lack of any other ideas, Sparrow wet a washcloth and placed it on her forehead. Elaina had gold flecks in her green eyes and freckles across the bridge of her nose. Sparrow had never noticed. In different circumstances, she could easily pass for an Emma.

"I would say you could crash with Grandma and me except we have even less room."

Elaina nodded but said nothing, for fear that she would cry.

Judy's long shift as cashier started well. It was rainy, so busier than usual, but Judy had memorized the script of greetings and thank you that the Episcopal ladies provided. By the sixth customer she could chat while she bagged and made change like she had been doing it for weeks. That's what the ladies themselves said. She was a natural. Then right after she had a bathroom break, Sparrow came in.

Sparrow had not been to the thrift shop since Monday, when Judy had watched her from the laundry room again. The Monday cashier had only charged two dollars for a skirt and blouse that were marked ten. Why would she do that except Sparrow was pretty and had gone on about her aged grandmother? It was intolerable.

Judy had sketched her confrontation with Sparrow in her imagination and played it out over and over. But it didn't go as planned. Sparrow came to the counter with a sequined black vest and long purple stockings. Judy was pleasant. She stuck with the script. She welcomed Sparrow to Sacred Heart, commented on how lovely the items were (the vest really was), and rang up the purchase: $15. Sparrow handed her five. Judy was strategic. She continued with the script, saying how everyone was asked to pay what they could or the sticker price. Sparrow replied that she was a regular customer and understood the arrangement. Judy then said, "So you are ten dollars short."

She expected Sparrow to blush. She expected her to hem and haw, fumble around in her wallet, and either pull out the correct amount or return the items to the rack.

Sparrow glared at her. "Do I have to show you my SNAP card? Or maybe I should phone up my blind grandmother and have her vouch for us?"

In Judy's imaginary scripts, there was a moment when she asked Sparrow why she wasn't working. Why someone her age, someone independent and pretty like her, couldn't at least get a waitressing gig. Did she think that Judy wasn't onto her game, buying low and selling high on the street? In her imaginary script, Sparrow blushed, flipped her off, and stormed out of the store.

"No, I don't need your SNAP card."

"Well, I'm going to show it to you anyway," Sparrow shouted. "Here. And let me phone Grandma. She keeps the TV loud so you'll have to speak up."

An Episcopal lady stepped out of the business office and offered assistance.

"Then," Judy said, as she told the story to Elaina, "that little hussy lied on me. Said that I had demanded to see her SNAP card. But Miss Eldridge had heard the whole thing and said that wasn't exactly accurate, but five dollars would be fine. It's not what I would have said, but never mind, because then the hussy said it ought to be free for all the humiliation she'd endured. Can you believe that? Even Miss Eldridge, who is too nice to begin with, wouldn't accept such nonsense. She said pay five dollars or please leave. I'm not going to repeat how she replied to that."

From the moment that Elaina recognized Sparrow as her mother's culprit, she wanted to stop her. Her mother paced and fumed like an evangelist. Even if Elaina could have found the words, what good would it do to say them? This is why, as her mother reached the final crescendo, Elaina went into her room, put on her checkerboard dress, and walked back to the kitchen table in silence.

"Where did you get that? We had one like it at Sacred Heart."

"I bought it from the hussy. Sparrow. That's her name. She is a friend of mine who runs a business online called Olivia's Oldstyle. I think it's genius. I gave her $25, and it was worth twice that much if you ask me."

"You paid $25? To that nasty girl?"

"Nasty girl? Are you in eighth grade?"

"Sparrow can't be her real name."

"She has an online business. People like her clothes."

"I could have brought that dress home to you for free."

"But you never would have, even if I had known about it and asked."

"How do you know? Besides, it's wrong what she's doing. She could have paid the sticker price and still made a profit."

"Why not make more?"

"What do you know about her, anyway? Since when did you become friends? She's no good. Why are you always attracted to people who are no good?"

"Right. So now you're going to put her and Hector in the same basket."

"And why not? Two of a kind. Shady. Working the system. Mark my word, if she's being friendly, there's a motive."

"Or maybe she just likes my company. You can't stand the thought of it."

"Mark my word. I warned you about your drug fiend boyfriend who got you pregnant, and now I'm warning you about a twiggy girl who's going to take you for a ride yet. If she don't end up in jail first."

Elaina thought about saying that that couldn't be worse than being trapped with Judy in the home for unwanted children. But she let it go. She closed herself up in the bathroom. She gazed at herself in the dress. She had a mind to buy another. Soon her belly would flatten and her breasts go back to normal. She snapped a photo to Sparrow. "See you tomorrow."

Sparrow did not come back to tea with Elaina. The judge believed that a lesson needed to be learned and gave her six months for misdemeanor assault. Elaina messaged her repeatedly but got no reply. New ensembles stopped appearing on Olivia's Oldstyle. Elaina had no idea where Sparrow lived, so she couldn't check on her.

Judy continued being cashier and couldn't find a tolerable solution for Mike's kids. Elaina made up her mind. As soon as she weaned the twins, she ran off and left them with Judy.

24

Girl With Owl, I

It came back to her as if tethered to her heart. So she could not bear to reject it even if she had no room and its daily tribute of slaughtered moles upset her. "There is no natural beauty without brutality," she whispered as she nodded thanks. Its wings enfolded her like feathered vestments. It became her eyes in the night.

Girl With Owl, II

Your gaze matches your bird's:
Beyond and back, de profundis,

Profess love in wordless titters,
Or a screech to rouse the torpid.

She was off her rocker, they said,
Carried mice for it in her trench coat.

Watched everyone, saw through everything.

Eastern Whip-Poor-Will

"Using multiple and independent monitoring networks, we report population losses across much of the North American avifauna over 48 years, including once-common species and from most biomes. Integration of range-wide population trajectories and size estimates indicates a net loss of approaching 3 billion birds, or 29% of 1970 abundance" (Rosenberg et al., 2019)

We stood by the canal at dusk
Waiting for the whip-poor-will
You heard in early summer.

Katydids, crickets, cicadas.
The dock's complaints.
A semi decelerated in the distance

And the harvest moon raked
Ripples on the surface
You'd fished often, with luck.

But from the loblolly pines
"Thick as hair on a dog's back,"
You couldn't coax a reply to your call.

Its song signals loneliness:
Two staccato notes then an octave's leap
To *will*, tapering, like a sigh.

How long before we notice loss,
The common sort, which is most of it,
Like the whip-poor-will we didn't miss

Until you heard one, first in a decade,
And we thought to wonder why.
You keyed the question into your phone.

It seems we poisoned their moths
To increase feed corn yields,
We clear-cut habitat to build suburbs.
So much destruction for hamburgers and lawns.

For two nights we listened, whispering,
Waiting, swatting mosquitoes,
"He might've eaten those," you laughed

Before we shrugged and gave up,
Hoped he found a mate farther south,
Not assuming we'd never hear another.

Common House Spider

(Parasteatoda tepidariorum)

1. Its scientific name

Misnamed "tepid," mildness is a lure.

"Look like th'innocent flower" or better

Be invisible, beige, fangs retracted:

By morning, three beetle domaldes.

2. Its web

Dog hair tumbleweed,

Tangled by design,

A fruit fly searches

For an opening.

Disrupted

(On the Hudson River at Kingston Point, 18 March 2020)

Four o'clock sun creeps across the surface
Of a low-tide labyrinth of pools and mudflats,
Glistening, charred, like foil from a barbecue.

Three turkey vultures meet on a heap
Of scrap timber and tires mired in the riverbed.
They spread their wings: panels to catch the rays.

They raise their blistered heads as if to sing,
Opening their beaks to clear their carrion throats.
But a vulture is songless as well as silent.

Fish crows cackle and dive at them,
More than a nuisance, less than a threat,
Like much of what we should ignore but don't.

So they catch the wind for a moment,
Sail upwards, circle once, twice,
Glide in a spiral back to their perch,

Death's cleanup crew: big, graceful,
Ugly and unflappable. Waiting.

Love Story With Birds

Chapter 1 Firebird, Previously Owned

Salesman said, "That's the cleanest undercarriage
You'll ever encounter," and "It takes
Less effort than what you previously owned."
They smiled.
Everything smelled of pine forest air freshener.

Chapter 2 Firebird, New Owners

A tiny flock flew when he removed her top,
Arcs of orange like solar flares in the backseat.

"Robins?" he asked, ignorant.
"Orioles," she sighed and pulled his belt.

"It didn't hurt?" he asked, touching lightly.
"I like orioles," she explained and bit.

Chapter 3 Starlings

"I'm missing the cake in this," she complained,
"And who decides you can't have it and eat it, too?"

They spoke of internal combustion and love
While she poured water in the radiator.

He nodded, "It's a stupid saying. Somewhere
There's always Kung Pao Chicken and Chocolate Yoohoos."

It was a hot day, noisy with starlings,
Iridescent wings like oil stains on the blue sky.

Chapter 4 At A Rest Stop By The Sea
"They fought mid-air," he said,
the old man. His teeth were gray.
He carried an impressive camera.

"The osprey tried to snatch
the carp from the eagle's talons."
He showed them the picture on the screen.

Beyond them, the dead fish floated,
Luminous at sunset.

Chapter 5 Lapwings

On the night road, they listened to *Wuthering Heights*.

In a scrape, an odd, antennaed plover broods,
Her black eye blinks now, and again now,
Against the wind and the pursuits
Of lovers who have pledged themselves

To perpetual motion and heat.

 "It's awful," he said, "how everyone
Smacks everyone for pure spite."
"What," she asked, speeding up,
"Is the purity of spite?"

As the Firebird caught air.

Ghost Variations

Under the left hand a solid,
Liquid under the right,
Sound travels along the skin
Like the lover's eyes.

Sorrow defies physics.
It is the stone and the water,
The river that embraces the body
And the weight that sinks it.

Schumann nodded at the angel.
His hands failing him,
His mind crumbling,
He composed for Clara,

Loved her, and knelt in shadow.

Note: In February 1854, Robert Schumann composed a set of piano variations on a theme sung to him by spirits. Shortly afterward, he attempted suicide in the Rhine.

Still

(Nov. 3, 2020-Jan. 30, 2021)

still (adv.)

In the days following the 2020 Presidential election—days of anxiety and dread that defined the year of the virus and Trumpism—I read the New York Times review of Barack Obama's memoir and longed for the former president. The Times reviewer noted that the two most frequent words in Obama's memoir were "maybe" and "still." Obama's penchant for these adverbs suggested that his hopefulness was nested in forethought. *Maybe things will turn out otherwise, still we should prepare.* Trump also loved a "maybe," but his equivocation pivoted on whether the outcome would keep him in the spotlight. *We'll see,* he would say, *maybe*, hedging because he had no substantive ideas about the topic in question. The difference between a Trump and Obama "maybe" or "still" is darkness and light.

For a momentary escape from the darkness at the end of 2020, I turned to Dickens. It had been many years since I last read *David Copperfield*, and I learned that it is still my favorite Dickens novel. My affinity for the novel may derive from Dickens' insistence that despite the welter of cruelty that defines social life, human goodness persists. David is essentially good, as are several of his adopted relations—not flawless, but giving and forgiving, the two qualities that in this instance define "good." There is a hazard that such goodness underwrites gullibility and will come to suffering. It's the dilemma that Dickens returns to over and over. His stories of children are variations on lamentations of disillusionment, which is not to say that disillusionment has the final word. Reflecting on his schooldays, David recalls his admiration and affection for an older schoolmate, Steerforth. Dashing and clever, egocentric and mendacious, Steerforth rules the boarding school and manipulates his admirers in ways that they are too young or too cowed to recognize. Dickens is a master of dramatic irony, and the brilliance of David's narration of his schooldays is that the child's perspective seems authentic even as we are aware that Steerforth is only in it for himself, where "it" is any relationship, occupation, transaction or commitment. In a climactic school days scene, Steerforth humiliates the teacher, Mr. Mell, who unlike most Dickensian schoolmasters deserves no humbling but is forced to admit before everyone that his mother lives in charity housing. Steerforth knows this from David, who told it to him innocently, but as Steerforth broadcasts it, Mr. Mell quietly pats David's hand. We cringe at Steerforth's cruelty and admire both Mr. Mell's compassion for David and his ability to see through Steerforth. Reflecting back on all of this as an adult, David muses on the fact that his disillusionment did not fully erase his feelings for Steerforth:

> There was an ease in his manner—a gay and light manner it was, but not swaggering—which I still believe to have borne a kind of enchantment with it. I still believe him, in virtue of this carriage, his animal spirits, his delightful voice, his handsome face and figure, and, for aught I know, of some inborn power of attraction besides (which I think a few people possess), to have carried a spell with him to which it was a natural weakness to yield, and which not many persons could withstand

I still believe, I still believe—David writes of enchantment, of being spellbound. The spell leaves a potent residue. How quickly memory reactivates it, breaking the stillness. David again feels that belief—the former delight, the admiration—despite what he knows. If only the confidence implied in Steerforth's name had been balanced by trustworthiness, he had been worth the persistence of David's belief in him.

I began writing this essay before January 6, 2021. "How can they still support him?" was already a refrain before senators and representatives were rushed into hiding as delusional protestors stormed the Capitol building in the name of Trump to disrupt the certification of the election. Returning from lockdown, many members of Congress still voted to overturn the election to keep Trump in power. Did they still believe in Trumpism? In my estimation, belief had nothing to do with the calculations of such cynics as Ted Cruz and Josh Hawley. Their votes could be explained by lust for power and an eye on the main chance. Their older leaders, Mitch McConnell, or Lindsay Graham, had the grace to be shaken by neo-Nazis and armed Christian nationalists breaking glass in the Capitol building and threatening to hang the Vice President. Even still, they'll only abandon Trump if it proves politically advantageous, as they signaled by reverting to obstructionism after the Senate changed hands. The party is powerless without Trumpism, so they'll go where it takes them. The greater puzzle has always been the true believers, who came out by the thousands on January 6. They accepted the conspiracy theories as a legitimate counter-narrative to the facts of the elections because for at least five years, they had trusted that Trump represented them. That he loved them. "We love you," Trump said to his followers after the failed insurrection, allaying any doubt that may have crept into their peripheral vision, their eyes fixed on the leader. Failure became success, loss became a lie. Even now, even tomorrow, they still believe.

still (n.)

"Still" as persistence over time implies the motion of the clock, night turning to day turning again to night. But it's motionlessness that connects the adverb and the noun, the stillness. "In the still of the night" crooned The Five Satins, dropping the "ness" for the sake of rhythm and gaining "the still," a poetic noun: In the still (shoo doop shooby doo) of the night (shoo doop shooby doo). The 1956 love ballad, which would return to the charts in 1987 with the *Dirty Dancing* soundtrack, is suggestive in a way that barely registers now when lyrics leave nothing to the imagination. "Hold me again / With all of your might / In the still of the night," Fred Parris pleads. This very tight holding needs to happen "before the light," under cover of darkness, under the stars. It's a doo wop aubade, warding off the sunrise as well as pleading for one more tumble. Rhythm in stillness, two anapests (in the still/of the night) broken by those doo wop iambs (shoo doop __ shooby doo). Let us linger on the genius of the blank that follows the staccato "doop," the pause on the unaccented syllable so that there is a release in "shooby doo." That syncopation, which depends on an empty space where a note was expected, makes the song. The longing for the night to continue is captured by stretching the lyric out. After each pause for the shooby doos, Parris comes in just before the beat, pulling us toward it, and closer to an ecstatic still point.

In meditation the mind is trained on stillness while it remains aware of motion. If you can find a quiet place, you will still experience distractions. Notice them, you are told, and return to the still point. In my favorite local used bookshop, I recently found a slim collection of essays by Thomas Merton called *Zen and the Birds of Appetite*. The size and raggedness of the copy was inversely pro-portional to the weight and beauty of Merton's reflections. Having studied Zen, Merton tried to reorient the Western Christian attitude of prayer away from petitions and requests and toward contemplation. There had been such modes of prayer in the early church, and Merton explained that it's not that Christians should give up one type for the other, but that without the silence and stillness of contem-plation, Christians could not fully experience the divine. Words, like noise and business, are barriers to the experi-ence. What he called "contemplative prayer" concentrates on the empty space. Paul Tillich, the theologian whose existentialism became a refuge to me in the first year of Covid-19, points to that space, the void, and argues that only in the full acknowledgement of meaninglessness, in that space of absolute stillness, can we affirm the purpose of what we say and do on this broken planet.

Maybe emptiness is stillness fully realized. Here is a familiar verse from the Tao Te-Ching, as translated by Red Pine: "pots are fashioned from clay / but it's the hollow / that makes a pot work." Emptiness is potential; emptiness invites substance. Before you fill the bowl, imagine all the things that could be poured in –water, oranges, buttons, memories, screams, tears. All insubstantial in the imagination but as real as a still life hanging before your mind's eye in your quiet room. You may never put a real orange there. You may put six or seven. Would they float in the tears? Burst in the screams?

still (n., from distill)

Had I not sat by the estuary, had I kept walking as I usually do when I'm looking for birds, I would not have seen the fox. A gray November midmorning, not the most inviting time to sit by the water, but on the rail along the river I needed a break from the pandemic mask. So I veered off, down by the waterside at low tide, and with my binoculars scanned the breakwater that leads to the lighthouse. Among the auburn reeds he was camouflaged—surely not a common condition for a red fox. Leggy and lithe he pranced along the edge, unnoticed by the gulls or herons that he must have considered dining on. Then again, how would I know his mind, or the birds' minds? None evidenced the least alarm, and the fox

tipped along until his redness was distilled into the desiccated reeds near the last buoy, the copper tones of late
autumn, of whiskey, of the kettle in the song that then
came to mind:

> I go to some hollow
>
> And set up my still
>
> And if whiskey don't kill me
>
> I don't know what will
>
> from "The Moonshiner," Roud 4301.

Drinking up the source of your revenue, aware that
taking the edge off is hardening your liver and shaving
cells off your brain, you do it anyway. The secrecy, what
you do alone in some dark hollow, is as much a sign of
your addiction as an evasion of the law. When my brother
and I were young, we found our grandfather's still disas-
sembled behind the hay in the barn. I don't know that he
ever sold his wares. I suspect he moonshined for his own
needs alone and found that he couldn't make it for the
price of a pint of Wild Turkey. I don't recall ever seeing
him drunk, but there were always empty bottles in the
burn barrel under the oak tree where he'd nailed a basket-
ball hoop for the children and grandchildren. Medicinal,
we were told. The suffering that leads to addiction, and
the addiction that leads to suffering, need daylight and
compassion. But whiskey goes down easier.

Hoping that the fox would rematerialize, I kept my

binoculars trained on the reeds until my arms grew weak with holding the same position. Then, as if sent by the Holy Spirit or the ghost of Gerard Manley Hopkins, a merlin swept across my periphery and lit on the highest branch of a cottonwood. My phone buzzed. Work. I had to take it. But as the intricacies of interdepartmental conspiracy theory unraveled in my ear, I watched the merlin, motionless, a sentinel. She will attack when the unsuspecting white-throated sparrows venture from the brush and onto the rail trail. I don't want to witness that. I accept the necessity of it but will be more troubled by the snatching of a little sparrow than had the fox taken down a gull. It's inexcusable, my sentimental bias for the "little," but I can't shake it.

Sympathy for the small is natural. But for the weak? Addiction is an embarrassing weakness. I was raised in a teetotalling Baptist community. One drank in the shadows. A coffee mug could obscure a few shots. God would know, but the family wouldn't. Spare them the shame. Evangelical Christianity is premised on the shame of giving into physical desire. Our weakness is sin. Jesus died for drunks like us. The dark hollow of the moonshine still, that place of secret sin that everyone knows about but turns away from: the path to it is down hill but to get out of it is a climb. Best not to go there in the first place.

A measure of how strong the pull is, of how the

desire becomes need, is that one gives into it despite such indoctrination. Hell for the evangelical alcoholic is not just the disintegration of his life, nor is it a metaphor. It is an actual eternal pit of fire and separation. Sin lands you there, you're warned, and drinking is sin. Still one slips off to the still. Evangelical Christianity fails to understand the psychology of addiction, or even the nature of suffering in solitude. Might as well direct the merlin to ignore the sparrows, or the fox to shed its redness, as to threaten an alcoholic with damnation.

still (v., trans.)

To distil, actually or figuratively, is common. But as a transitive verb, still belongs only in poetry now. "How to calm your baby" is advice sought by a new parent. But in the "stille nacht, heilige nacht," Mary didn't wonder how to still her baby, who, we are told, was tender and mild and supernaturally complaisant. As a child I was told to "get still," and as a parent I've probably used that command. But I never ordered one of the boys, "still your body." According to the OED, using "still" to denote "lull, soothe (a child)" is obsolete, the latest example being from 1660, "He would still his Nephewes when they cryed with plums," Francis Brooke translating the French explorer Vincent Le Blanc's *The World Surveyed*. What nephew in the 21st century, at least in the US, would be stilled by plums? Fruit is too healthy to work as a bribe, and the skin of a plum will make your nephew shudder. You'll have to peel and slice it, then you'll have sticky fingers and drips on your good trousers. And I doubt that your nephew would sit still for it, let alone stop whining.

I should point out that the uncle in Le Blanc's travel tale has the entertaining advantage of being an ape, whose human nephews are charmed as much by his apishness as his fruits. Traveling in Abyssinia, Le Blanc hears the story of a young Prince Joel, whose father dies and whose stepmother, wishing the legacy to pass to her own children, sends Joel to her sorceress sister "out of a frantick malice." The Sorceress is prepared to sacrifice the child to Satan, but being moved by the boy's sweet face, she instead concocts a magical bath that turns him into an ape. Coming from a Christian family, Joel has a guardian angel, who proves powerless to intervene with the wicked stepmother and even more wicked aunt. But in time the angel does manage to bring the monkey Joel into contact with his brother, who is traveling in stately array through the wilderness. As an ape, Joel is of course not recognized, but he shows remarkable promise as a cupbearer and is taken back to court, where he works many wonders including, as we know, plying recalcitrant nephews with plums. A princess cousin becomes especially fond of Joel. In the still of the night, she is visited by a vision of her aunt, Joel's true mother, who reveals Joel's identity to her and gives her herbs for a bath that restores Joel to human form.

Le Blanc describes the story as "Tragie-Comedie" and seems not to doubt its authenticity, given his personal experiences with magical transformations on his many journeys. 400 years from now, if the United States still exists, what will be the genre of the narrative of 2020? "Tragicomedy" is inappropriate, because in spite of the fact that Trump legitimately lost the election, the year did not end with the happy resolution of comedy. "Morality tale" won't do. No God intervened to save America from itself despite the national confidence that God blesses America, and too many of the worst offenders are still in power. I am inclined to go with "tragedy": the flaw in the national character led to multiple fatalities; the sins of its founding required penance but garners little in the way of penitence; the faith in the Constitution blinded us to its fragility. But even without the hindsight of 400 years, tragedy seems too high-minded for any drama that starred Donald Trump, despite the tragic consequences of his actions and those of his enablers. I have been accused of being sentimental about the nation's fate. There is more of Beckett than Dickens about the first year of the pandemic and the Trumpian circus. Maybe 2020 was theatre of the absurd.

still (adj.)

I have never sailed in a storm. But the metaphor of choice in the media of 2020 put us there repeatedly. Another wave of the virus, its surges and swells. The sea of protestors, the nation plunged into violence. In America, where individual desire trumps collective good, we're bailing water to keep our bark from sinking.

Around Christmas 2020, ten months into the pandemic, a few weeks into the post-election turbulence stirred up by Trump and his minions, I reread the tale from the Gospel of Mark. "Peace, be still." The King James Version is worth quoting in full, because the beauty of the narrative is in the details of that translation:

> 35 And the same day, when the even was come, he saith unto them, Let us pass over unto the other side. 36 And when they had sent away the multitude, they took him even as he was in the ship. And there were also with him other little ships. 37 And there arose a great storm of wind, and the waves beat into the ship, so that it was now full. 38 And he was in the hinder part of the ship, asleep on the pillow: and they awoke him, and said unto him, Master, carest thou not that we perish? 39 And he arose,

and rebuked the wind, and said unto the sea, Peace, be still. And the wind ceased, and there was a great calm. 40 And he said unto them, Why are ye so fearful? How is it that ye have no faith? 41 And they feared exceedingly, and said one to another, What manner of man is this, that even the wind and the sea obey him?

Scholars note the quick pace and parataxis of Mark's gospel, everything joined by "and" and "and," to paraphrase Elizabeth Bishop's great poem about a biblical concordance. That forward motion mirrors the apostles' agitation, in contrast with Jesus, "asleep on a pillow" in the stern. Why that detail: the pillow? It's not that he's just nodded off after a long day of sermonizing. He has turned in. Note that a crowd had pressed him and his disciples onto the boat, from which he spoke parables about the kingdom of God—the sower, the mustard seed. Simple fishermen, his disciples couldn't quite decipher his metaphors, so the sermon was followed by private lessons in hermeneutics. We're told that, "alone, he expounded all things to his disciples." It was exhausting work, so much so that he's sleeping through a storm that threatens to sink his ship and several others.

Tribulations shake the people of faith and their master rebukes them. Faith the size of a mustard seed should still the agitated soul. Paul Tillich defined faith as having an ultimate concern. It drives the faithful forward, but in its stability, it is also the space of rest when things are falling apart. The disciples' master calms the storm and the disciples. Peace, be still. But the master's point is that he won't always be around to speak those words. The faithful have to speak them on their own. They must create the stillness in the middle of the storm—the calm in which a plan can be implemented.

In the US, we lacked such frank but caring leadership during the greatest national crisis of the 21st century. Trumpism will not fade away even if its figurehead is brought to justice. Still, we gain nothing by conceding to our fears and the worst impulses of our national character. We perpetuate suffering by scrolling our social media feeds in mounting agitation, or dismissing hope with a skeptic's panache, or mouthing it without feeling in the manner of our republic's most cynical leaders. The spokes of a wheel come together at the hub, wrote Lao-Tzu, but the emptiness is essential to its work. Still the body. Contemplate the facts and feelings. Act on behalf of another. Maybe we are better than the evidence suggests.

Vigil

He was a cobweb in the chair.
His coughs broke him.
I did nothing. There was nothing
to do but hold my breath
while he panted himself whole again.

"To think is to be full of sorrow."

Keats willed words not to fail him,
He held his brother
who withered ghostward.
His stare had no horizon.
It was infinite. It was empty.

Note: John Keats nursed his brother as he died of tuber-
culosis, the disease that would also kill the poet. The line
is from "To A Nightingale."

Jolene

When the grandkitten slipped out I was
listening to Lady Bird Johnson's tapes while
weeding the hedges—thankless beautification,
not worth losing a cat. For hours
we crawled under neighborhood porches and called
"Jolene!", pitiful, like that Dolly Parton ballad,
"I'm begging of you please don't take my man."
Corny like that, too, from a secure vantage point,
as when your cat's safe on your lap and your man's
only gone to the kitchen for a beer after gardening.
Temporary idyll: domestic bliss follows an arc
that bends toward sorrow before it snaps.
Consider Frankenstein's creature. He peers
through a chink at a happy forest family,
he longs for the joys of domesticity,
risks a conversation with the blind grandfather.
Then the children return. We hate what happens next
but we know how stories go for monsters,
misunderstood and abused like a long-suffering partner.
That's all the creature asks of his creator:
a lover, hearth of his own, a closed arctic circle.
Of course someone would have slipped in
or slipped out while he did the chores.
Lady Bird, beautifier, helpmate,

stood by her philanderer like Jackie before her,
and Eleanor, probably even Martha.
Ladies wore gloves, hats with veils,
closed-toe high heels, and guarded secrets.
Jolene, sleek, vilified, walks on the edge,
Catwoman-nimble, her delicate toes exposed.
There's a war on, whispers the first lady,
the country's in flames, keep it
in your trousers, it's patriotic.
"Don't take him from me," Dolly begs,
"Just because you can."
Why did you dash away from us, Jolene?
Was the home we made not enough?
Pathos is a predator, the heart is a mouse.
The king dies, the queen dies of grief.
That's plot, EM Forster said, but in my unwritten novel
the queen finds someone new, takes the cat
to an island to set up shop, bait and tackle,
plays her cello on the pier every sunset for the lovers.
If only Victor had followed through,
cared for his child and given him a girlfriend,
or the creature had stolen his master's fire
and made a companion on his own.
But Mary—the second woman, pregnant,
in love with a modern Prometheus,
alone in a damp Italian villa while

Percy and Byron philandered,
her first child dead, the woman she replaced
(Harriet) drowned in the Serpentine—
Mary couldn't write that story.

Aphorisms

He was a gas leak, creaky stairs,
red flags unfurling, a sty in your lashes.
He burned the roof of your mouth.
When we heard he was in prison again,
we sighed with his grandmother,
"You can't love them too hard
because they never get enough."

His daughter was broken glass.
We couldn't sweep all of her up.
Before she set the apartment on fire
and took to the street for good,
she zipped the cat inside her parka
to keep it close.
                    "It rains every day
till it starts snowing," the grandmother said.
"So take the relief you're offered."
She wore yellow feathers in a roach clip
and never walked if there was a bus.
If you meet her, say yes to the slice of gum.

Hedge

Braided into the honeysuckle that chokes the hedge
You've chosen to trim today under full sun
And with a fool's determination to finish quickly,
A garter snake unlaces the vines and slips
Yellow blades across the greenest new growth
To open a portal into which it plunges.

There might be, for all you know, a space
Of undisturbed joy beneath its disappearance,
One that accommodates delight such as this—
The finding of little serpents—and welcomes
Dawdlers who settle for description:
Sleek surety, black curl, delicate ancient tongue.

The Fox

As I hurry on
75 mph down the Northway in the night
I imagine you before your death:

We are near the High Peaks.

You trot to the wood's edge.

The opening onto the black stretch of highway extends
To the Milky Way and the crescent moon,
A lash of light.

You are not red in the dark.
Your white tips and your eyes flicker.

I imagine you confident,
Unfazed by the black expanse,
Wading into it when sudden
Headlights blind you and
You freeze.

Poor Jack

My son and his mother wept when Jack died
in *By the Shores of Silver Lake*. It was fall.
I came home from teaching fifth grade.
They were collapsed on the couch,
Sammy was five, red-haired and plump,
trembling, wedged under Caroline's wing.
She sobbed and stroked his back, and I
dropped my bag at the door, I was numb
with fear, "Who had died? *Our* dog?"
Outside the beeches were bronze, the wood thrush
had not yet migrated, winesaps were ripe.

It was a dress rehearsal, if an unexpected one,
like the faulty smoke alarm, angina, the missed curfew
that could be a car wreck. Everyone has them,
often through a book: prairie fires, scarlet fever,
or as in *Anna Karenina*, when she regrets,
too late, that she has bowed down in darkness.
I saw this coming, knew it the second time,
and I teared up in spite of the foreknowledge,
or because of it, who knows?
                        Today,
two dogs later, we are on the same green couch,
dilapidated now. We laugh to remember

boohooing mother and son, flummoxed father,
poor Jack (*such a sad story!*) while
sickness sweeps the country, the Dow
plummets, hospitals and morgues surge,
prophets warn, "He'll steal the election
again." Then Caroline recalls, "I was
pregnant on 9/11—eight months—
so was the bagel shop girl,
What are we doing, she asked me
through her tears as she made change,
bringing children into this?"
                              Out our window
a masked boy pedals his tricycle.
His masked mother stops to admire
our lawn full of bluebells.
Sammy answers his phone in Japanese,
smiles (the girlfriend) and dashes upstairs.
Gabby (the dog) grunts.
Czeslaw Milosz wrote
that on the day the world ends, an old man
binding tomatoes repeats, "There will be no other
end of the world." It was midsummer,
in Warsaw, 1944. People like to point out
it was sunny on 9/11, it's Passover and Easter
for the pandemic, it may be Happy Thanksgiving
for Armageddon. Poor Jack,

we're curled up on the couch with the ideal
of you, of how your people loved you
by their fireside, how they huddled
under a blanket and imagined the worst
and remembered the best.

--April 2020

The Hydra

During that rainy summer, ants moved inside.
We went in circles trying to stop them:
Wiped out a squadron, cleaned the counter,
turned out the lights, more materialized.
We could see why people accepted
spontaneous generation, why philosophers
argued with Leeuwenhoek until animalcules
loomed before them under his microscope.
You need magnification and persistence
to get to the bottom of things.
Those tiles are sterile, but not flawless.
Upon closer scrutiny, you'll find a crack,
maybe several obscure portals where
trouble seeps in.
                  I still prefer
maps to GPS, I want the journey
spread out before me in symbol and scale,
orientation to the spaces I won't cross as well as
the place I'm standing. The little lady
in my phone never fails to know precisely
where I should turn, still it seems like
blind faith to listen without checking the map,
as if I were a monk with the rosary or
a Greek hero taking cues from Aphrodite.

But the lady's eyes are sharp, her vista
wide. "Just trust her for god's sake,"
my son the computer scientist implores.
With the lady or the map what's the worst
that can happen—a right rather than a left,
an unintended detour where you see
a street you would otherwise miss,
lawns of tin animals on no map,
a deli called Arcadia?
                    Once at a traffic light
a guy and his girlfriend jumped into my car.
He was jonesing, demanded to be driven
to his friend's deli. She chatted cheerily,
wedging herself between the child booster seats,
asked if I had kids. I said, "Boys, three and five."
"Bet you're a good dad," she sighed.
He changed his mind and said, "Fuck it,
how about $60, just a loan," and she laughed,
"You only now met him!" I lied that I didn't
carry cash and steered us toward a busy street.
"Find an ATM!" he shouted, coming down hard,
slapping the dashboard, reaching
under his jacket then pausing. She said,
"Just drop us there," pointing to a garage, "his cousin
owns it." He muttered, "Yes Richie, Yes Richie," until
I stopped and she said, "Thanks!" like the teenage cashier

at the ice cream parlor, and they piled out
into the darkness. When I saw them again a month later
they did not recognize me, or pretended not to,
it's impossible to say, I looked away. They were
holding hands.

        "Bhikkus, I say that getting rid of
troubles and cares," declared the Buddha, "is possible
for one who knows and who sees." But it's hard to see,
let alone know. In ninth grade biology my partner and I
found a budding hydra in a drop of pond water.
Amy saw it, I had missed it, being caught up
in note-taking and the scent of her shampoo.
A line formed at our microscope, no one
was too cool to look. Our hydra had
five arms and a mini-hydra like a navel.
Tiny protozoa too small to identify
whizzed by. Miss Hewitt taught us
Hercules was losing his battle,
snake heads spontaneously regenerated
as soon as he sliced one off until
his nephew, Iolaus, holding the light for him,
shoved his torch into the headless necks.
There is always more to understand
if you get closer and brighten
the light, persist and magnify.
Even still you'll stare right at

a tentacled marvel without seeing it.
So why not listen to the lady,
she is trying to direct you,
maybe get you out of a tight fix,
and her vision is 20/20.

In My Room

(With Jane Austen, Brian Wilson and Chantal Akerman During the Pandemic)

During much of the pandemic's first wave, I taught classes and held meetings, ate lunch and made coffee, commented on my students' essays and wrote my own all in a single room. I was fortunate to have such a room in my home—small, but with an Internet connection and books. Day and night, work and home were one place. Closed off to other bodies, my study nonetheless hosted more students and colleagues than ever. They've all seen the rickety bookshelf (it collapsed during a meeting) and children's drawings. I've seen their browning plants and Depeche Mode posters. Alone in our rooms, our isolation in the pandemic involved a constant stream of pixelating faces with attenuated voices. They arrived on schedule, disembodied. They did not so much take us elsewhere as remind us of the distance.

The sense of sameness during the pandemic, of nothing happening in spite of the constancy of business and tragedy, was reinforced by the narrow vista of the screen. In my room, I looked at, talked at, and gestured toward the 13 inches of my laptop screen for hours and hours. Days began and ended in a blue blur without a clear arc—"everything only connected by 'and' and 'and,'" as Elizabeth

Bishop wrote. Not that drama requires an uphill struggle to a peak, despite what we learned from our ninth-grade plot diagrams. Think of a typical scene from Jane Austen. Gathered in the parlor of a country house, women speculate on the new neighbor's wealth and relations, ruminate on the wisdom of a turn around the garden despite the dampness, or read about gothic heroines abducted to castles. They imagine the real plot is elsewhere, not in the spaces that they occupy. But for Austen's readers, the drama is in the dialogue—the wit, the innuendo, the sentence that reveals a character's perceptiveness or lack of it. An Austen plot turns on what is unsaid or overheard among three or four people in a room.

One of the great climactic moments in English fiction takes place in a small seaside home at a writing desk, where Captain Wentworth of *Persuasion* secretly pens a letter to Anne Elliott while she and Captain Harville debate whether men or women suffer the most when they are forced to be apart. Harville and Anne agree on one point: everyone wants to return to the hearth and their family's arms. Desperate for Anne, Wentworth writes the same sentiments just a few feet away, little knowing that she is equally desperate for him. The confined space is essential to the dramatic irony. It's 1815, Wentworth and Harville are both naval officers. What no one in the room or inside the novel's plot can foresee is that Napoleon will soon escape Elba, and war will resume. Anne's "dread of a future war," says the narrator in the final sentences of the novel, was all that could "dim her sunshine" after their marriage.

Confinement breeds dread. We perceive trouble on untroubled surfaces. We fix unbroken things. I became obsessed with the untidiness of my desk. Where did all those paper clips come from? Why is there never enough shelving? There is always dust. During the darkest days of the pandemic, my lamplight swirled with lint, as if I worked in a cotton mill. I could feel my hands shedding layers of my former self onto the keyboard—such a filthy space. I took to cleaning at least once per day. It was a break that gave the illusion of productivity. I could listen to music while I picked hairs from the rug. That's what I was doing when Spotify cued up the Beach Boys tune, "In My Room."

Over somnambulant guitar arpeggios, Wilson's sleepy vocals describe a teenage fantasy. The room is a sealed echo chamber, self-affirming and escapist. But all is not well. "Now it's dark and I'm alone," Wilson worries, and tells himself, "But I won't be afraid." Why the future tense? Why not a declaration in present tense: *But I am not afraid*? Anxiety is fed by solitude and darkness. It inflects the "dreaming" and "scheming" that Wilson sings of in the second verse. As with several lyrics in which Wilson had a hand, "In My Room" isn't all sunny Beach Boys harmony.

Among the many inequities laid bare by the pandemic was the difference in who has a private space. If you are a teacher, you know young people who had no choice but to join class by muted phone with camera off because the only "private" space in their home was the bedroom shared with siblings. There are many variations on that theme. The single computer shared by the entire family was in the common space, so everyone in the home could see, hear, and sometimes respond to the instructor and classmates. The Internet was so poor in the home that the student joined class, masked, from outside a business with a free WiFi hotspot. Or the students had to log off after being counted present because there were too few minutes on their family's calling plan. "In my room," where the personal possessive pronoun indicates sovereignty as well as solitude, signals a level of economic privilege enjoyed by too few young Americans. Not enough shelving is a problem anyone would wish to have.

To create room without a room requires determination and discipline over the senses. My mother could read with the television blaring *Laverne and Shirley* and *Good Times* and her children playing rocket ship under the table. She had grown up with seven people in a 3½-room house. As a teenager, whether she was reading Paul's letter to the Philippians or her school textbooks, she had to filter out my grandfather watching *Gunsmoke* and the hurly-burly of multiple brothers. When I turned 13, she cleared the sewing room and made me a bedroom of my own. Our modest brick ranch was a luxury home compared to the houses of her childhood, but there was still no escaping the television and family traffic unless you could shut a door and turn on radio static as white noise. That became my technique. I felt guilty about it, like a snob toward my family. But how else was I to concentrate on the algebra and the Shakespeare that, I was told, would get me to college and away from home? I stayed in my room, making preparations.

At my writing desk during the pandemic, in front of the inevitable screen in the same room for hours, I was pulled into the work of the Belgian filmmaker Chantal Akerman. Akerman mastered the long take, and the action, such as it is, often unfolds in a single space—a bedroom, a motel room, a truck cab. For instance, in *Dis Moi*, a documentary of interviews with elderly Jewish women who survived the Holocaust, Akerman simply lets her subjects speak as they sit on the couch or eat dinner. The child of survivors, she rarely asks a question or intervenes, as if to do so would be to wrest control from a storyteller whose narrative had already been circumscribed by tyranny and trauma. In *Je, Tu, Il, Elle*, a woman, played by Akerman, empties her Spartan apartment and sits on the edge of a mattress for hours. We cannot read her opaque countenance. We watch her eat sugar from a bag for minutes on end. It is an affecting portrait of depression precisely because Akerman's voiceover says almost nothing, and her camera stares at inaction. In two of her feature films, *Les Rendezvous d'Anna* and *Jeanne Dielman*, we watch food preparation, sex, escalator rides, and even murder with the same steady, dispassionate gaze. The love of a daughter for her mother, the love between women, the commitment of women to their undervalued work—like Austen, Akerman represents spaces that are uniquely and powerfully female.

In the immobilizing context of the pandemic, I found her most instructive film to be an early short, *La Chambre*. Akerman invites us into a room and dares us to make a story. The entire film takes place, without sound, in a small Parisian efficiency apartment. On a fixed point, the camera rotates 360 degrees, slowly, like a lighthouse, and we look out from it. The room is cluttered: a sink filled with dishes, a rack of scarves, an askew wall calendar, and the leftovers of coffee and pastries. When the camera's gaze approaches a window, the clutter is overexposed;

when it lights on a corner, we're in shadows. Overall the scene is grainy and flat, even when the gaze lands on a colorful item—a red wire chair with a valentine heart for its back, a small spinning wheel, a bulky lamp with an orange elephant painted on its base. Given the pace and the fact that the camera remains in one place, we're sometimes close to the wall for so long that we feel claustrophobic. But as we approach the end of the first scan of the room, the gaze falls on a woman (the director) in bed. She is looking at us. She moves her head side to side, robotically, like the camera's steady turning. It's just enough of a gesture to cause us to ask not only who she is but also what she is doing.

We anticipate her return as the camera creeps on. With the second pass, she has slid under the covers. Still looking at us, she now moves methodically, and as we begin to imagine what's happening beneath the sheets, the camera leaves her again. At the third return she has taken an apple from the bedside table. She's turning it, looking at it. Then shortly after leaving her again, the camera reverses direction. Finally, it seems, our eagerness to make this a story about the woman has been acknowledged. She's licking the apple now, and looking at us. The camera reverses again, and she's eating the apple voraciously. There's another reversal, the camera's pace has quickened. But the apple is already gone. The woman rubs her face repeatedly, as if exhausted or depressed, and lies back down. The camera moves past her and goes black.

In miniature, *La Chambre* has the intriguing sparseness and patience of Akerman's mid-70s features. It is a brilliant examination of narrative stripped to the minimum: single setting, single controlled perspective, single character, the slightest of events that nonetheless initiates a plot. The pacing calls attention to a consciousness that is not necessarily concerned about what we want, and yet when the camera reverses course, the seeming response to our interests, our desires, is a reminder that plot depends both on the maker and on the one receiving it. This is not our story, it is not our telling. Left to our own devices, we would linger on the woman. Even still, this short sparse study of a room is what we make of it.

How plot happens is the subject of *La Chambre*, so the camera's motion constantly occupies us. At the same time, the film is a still life. The motionless objects of the room are the film's content. We're asked to observe them closely, repeatedly. Their stillness in the pallor weighs on us. They are a counterpoint to the woman, whom we sensationalize as we're drawn to interpretation. We want to make more of the apple, of her eating it. Is this the Fall, are we being tempted? But the camera brings us back to the facts of the room, its unkempt state and greyness. Then it abruptly turns off.

Most of life is just so. It is sameness. We grow restless for plot. We manufacture intrigue from quotidian occurrences. Then an end arrives.

The setting of our lives is a mere handful of rooms. Choose one that rises to the top of the list—an office, a bedroom—and imagine yourself there. Pivot on a single point, rotating slowly, such that it takes a full five minutes to complete the circle. Your memory will fail you. Wasn't there a chair in that corner? What titles were visible on the shelf? When did the cactus arrive? Days upon days you sat on that couch and yet you cannot name its shade of green. You loved apples in the autumn. There were always a few in a basket. What kind were they?

I shouldn't overstate the significance of the unnoticed or unremembered. Sharp outlines blur with distance. But we need art and artists to help us see the room while we're in it. What we notice matters because there is otherwise little meaning in the day and none after it's ended. Akerman's *La Chambre* becomes a narrative as we react to the smallest gestures. Like any important work of narrative art, the film alerts us to the possibilities of the everyday. Even in times of crisis—perhaps especially in wars and pandemics—everything is only connected by "and" until our interest intervenes and we become concerned. If "the king died, then the queen died of grief" distills the nature of plot, as E.M. Forster argued, it's the reader, following the author's lead, who decides to look closely at the queen's state of mind and heart.

The artist guides our eye to the clutter of the room and the quality of light on the apples, and we wonder. She attunes our ear to the scratch of the pen hurrying to write the most earnest supplications before self-consciousness takes over. Surely the fact that I worry means something. Surely my room of so many days holds stories worth setting down. Consequence is an act of imagination. Everyone wants to imagine a consequential life.

Sweetest in the Gale is Heard

Deep Down Things

I watched an osprey as he fished near the lighthouse at Kingston Point in New York. He pulled up from a glide into an arc. His neck craned down, he beat his broad wings, hovering. This was the pattern for several minutes over the confluence of the Rondout Creek and Hudson River, where shad rolled the water. Twice he broke from the hover and dove, coming up empty the first time, quivering as he ascended to shake off the water and frustration. The second time he brought up a fish as large as his own body. He struggled to get airborne while the fish writhed in his claws. The fish won, though it fell from about 20 feet up. The osprey kept climbing, then took a wide, gliding turn over the area. He seemed to be recollecting himself before he settled back to the work of fishing. When I left, he was still at it, glaring at the river and pounding his wings.

For the osprey, as for most birds out in the early morning, this labor—the hunt for food—defines much of life. The creature is built for that purpose, second only to reproduction in importance. As he fishes, the osprey is fully present—being and doing are inseparable—and if I think "so persistent!", I do him an injustice. He has not reflected on failure and decided to continue. He has simply continued since survival depends on it.

What of my observing? What is the purpose of my being here, doing that? There is joy, all the greater for the live observation than had it come from a video or a book. When I walk on the waterfront, I anticipate such joy. But that's more the promise of the walk than its purpose. At least one reason that I come here is to shed unawareness. It takes a while. Wrapped in thought, nagged on by my phone which notifies me of nothing worth attending to over and over, I could easily miss a giant masked raptor, let alone the thousands of creatures that in this same place and time are searching, hunting, hiding, feeding, all with a degree of concentration that shames my dis-tractibility. As I tire of observing and become anxious about time passing (shouldn't I be doing something more productive?), the osprey keeps at it, indifferent to time and oblivious to me though I do not doubt he had noted me on the periphery and counted me unthreat-ening. Animals are nearly always aware of us and have calculated their response before we realize they're near, assuming we ever do.

Becoming aware of a fraction of the lives above, below, and around us, of the other creatures not just experiencing but making the world, shrinks the ego. Our ambitions and concerns swirl around us like a personal dust devil. We blow along disturbing sparrows and oblivious to katydids and assuming that man (sic) is the measure of all things. Not that as a rule, we're conscious of the needs of other people. Think about W. H. Auden's brilliant interpretation of the Brueghel painting, "Landscape with the Fall of Icarus." Icarus' death matters to Icarus and presumably to Daedelus, but it doesn't register with the person "just walking dully along" or to his dog, whose lives signify more to them than the falling boy. They don't see him, or if they do, they soon forget. Stuck in four lanes of traffic, we curse our luck. We have so far to go before we stop for the day, and we can't even see around the truck ahead to find out what's holding us up. We get frustrated. We play with the radio. We slap the steering wheel and peer out the window. Eventually we pass the smashed minivan and the ambulances and cops. There is a flicker of shame. Those were people, going somewhere, too. They had plans for tomorrow. We really hope no one died. Someone turns down the music, at least until the traffic clears.

The creature you stop to observe—that particular osprey, on that June morning—is full in its specificity. The life not yours in the landscapes you occupy is vast. Go beyond your small patch, and the scale seems inconceivable. What is your obligation to try to conceive of it?

In the pandemic, awareness of other human lives and their suffering involved conceiving of a scale that stretched our limited capacity. Even if politics had not distorted our vision, Americans may never have responded appropriately to the difference between 10,000, 100,000, or a million. In a series of studies, Paul Slovic and his colleagues described the human tendency to sympathize more with the one than the many. An image of a single desperate child is more likely to yield a practical response than a plea attached to masses of children. Recall Alan Kurdi, the three-year-old Kurdish-Syrian refugee who drowned when the raft carrying his family capsized five minutes into their journey. His body was photographed on a Turkish beach after being pulled from the water. The pathos of the image—his smallness, his being alone—led to story upon story and did more to elevate US and European consciousness (however temporarily) regarding the crisis in Syria than all the coverage to that point. We must have known that there were thousands like Alan, suffering and dying in conditions not of their making. But the one body in a red shirt, curled face down in the surf, the soles of his shoes upturned…a body that soon had a name and a story wouldn't let us turn away. Why would video of thousands of refugees in similar distress—the kind of video that had become a regular part of the news cycle—be any less effective in galvanizing all of us on our sofas to act? Slovic shows that even increasing the number from one child to two children affects our capacity for compassion. A sense of futility sets in as we question how effective our small contribution could be in addressing a need that seems to be perpetual and ever increasing.

In *Regarding the Pain of Others*, Susan Sontag writes that when people in a privileged position react to an image of suffering, there is a danger that they may not recognize their role in it. However well-intended, sympathy may be "an impertinent—if not an inappropriate—response."

There is the video of George Floyd's murder. There are the stills of people clinging to a plane as it departs Kabul airport. Each has become a synecdoche—for Black lives, for the victims of empire. They are vast, larger than the single life. But one of the most powerful gestures to arise from BLM protests after Floyd's death was "Say Their Names," followed by a litany of invocations of individual lives—Ahmaud Arbery, Breonna Taylor, Rayshard Brooks. The chant demanded particularity, not to deny the symbolic weight that Floyd's image, for instance, had gathered, but to sustain the individual's particular life a little longer than the breath that was taken from them. It is not impertinent to meditate on a particular life that has been rendered symbolic—on the life, not the symbol. Zaki Anwari, a member of the Afghan youth soccer team. Fada Mohammed, a dentist from the outskirts of Kabul.

At sunrise a daddy longlegs was trying to scale the steel slope of our kitchen sink. I needed water for coffee and didn't want to drown him. How to help him escape without crushing a delicate leg? I stood in a fog, kettle in hand, the non-arachnid spidery insect tumbling repeatedly toward the drain.

Flash back two weeks to my worst recent interaction with the creatures that share our home. The story that I'm about to relate brings me pain and embarrassment. We have an old Tupperware salad spinner. I took it from the cabinet and put it in the sink to prepare to wash a handful of lettuce. When I removed the lid, there sat a mouse. I started back, the plastic bowl tipped, and the mouse tumbled into the sink. It froze, and without a single thought, as if my arm were on a spring, I whacked it with the lid. What manner of beast am I beneath this vegetarian, animal-rights exterior? How simple to have scooped it back into the salad spinner and put it outside? Even simpler to have let it thaw and scurry off, to be caught later in the little gray humane traps we have for that purpose. I lay awake that night worried that I have hidden tendencies toward violence. I have no doubt that the mouse was a conscious being with desires and perceptions. Didn't it long for food, wish to remain alive, imagine—so briefly—an escape? Killing it without good reason (and such a reason would be hard to produce under the circumstances) is marginally different from slaughtering a pig and worse than squashing a bug—itself an act that should not be automatic. We're not automatons, and neither are insects.

Hence my dilemma at the sink. Shaking my head to clear the fog, I found a sheet of printer paper for the daddy longlegs to tiptoe onto, and I lifted him to the floor. That simple. No one died. Coffee was delayed by less than two minutes.

The death of that mouse, the life of that insect: I want to believe that attention to the smallest lives in our midst, maybe even a little curiosity about those lives for their own sake, will be disruptive. It could be an antidote to the toxins in the air as authoritarianism rises again, with its love of generalizations and platitudes. Our capacity to care for the human is adumbrated when we are careless about the nonhuman. "And for all this, nature is never spent," Hopkins wrote. "There lives the dearest freshness deep down things." We might call Hopkins' freshness the germ of a soul. In the US, the soul has been coopted by a subset of reactionary Christians and dismissed without reflection by a subset of the college-educated. The rest of us tend to ignore it altogether unless asked if we believe we have one. In his lectures on death, the Yale philosopher Shelly Kagan addresses each of Plato's arguments for the soul in the *Phaedo* and concludes that none is satisfactory when measured against the physicalist perspective. A body doesn't need a soul, but a person needs a body. Looking for the person, Kagan argues, "follow the body." When I watch an osprey, I wonder if belief in souls diminishes respect for bodies, human and other, all of which have evolved to states of glorious complexity that no human laboratory can approximate. And yet it's just such complexity, which manifests in personality and feeling and intention, that drives me back to "soul." I want a word, a large word with a history, for what moves when I finally listen to the evening resonant with creatures calling to each other, or for what stings when I see a fellow creature senselessly cut down. To imagine a soul is as good a way as any to encapsulate why, when we do finally regard the joy or suffering or simply the daily life of another, we feel a connection and, however fleetingly, a responsibility.

Sunday's List

Aubade: Mourning Dove
Appeared to us.
Imagine a door opens.
Folded linen, a breeze,
Disturbance and joy.

Tree Swallows
Apoplectic, fidgety in line,
A row of first grade boys, until
They dive down and skim the surface
Of the sunlit morning river, hunting.

Yellow Warblers
Exuberant, unabashed.
Scarlet stretch marks,
Their tiny bellows bulge.

Common Yellowthroat
Why not "masked warbler"?
This one skulks in marsh grass.
Its mate in olive drab lets
Show a golden neckerchief.

      Two Mute Swans
      Their quietness, the drifting
      By cattails. It is overcast,
      Someone fishes for shad.

Twelve Grackles
The red oak
Dripping tassels, filtering light.
The grackles' yellow eyes:
Distillate.

Sharp-Shinned Hawk
It peels from the hemlock bark.
Sparrows bicker in the spilled millet.
When they scatter it's too late.

Marsh Wren
I waded through poison ivy to see you.
Invisible you did not move.
You sang and sang among the cattails.
Failing I was not unhappy.

Ring-Billed Gulls
They leap up, hover, and descend,
Changing order on the sandbar, the trawler
Muttering in the fog, staining it diesel.

And they squawk shamelessly,
A joyful noise, because joy is shameless.

Chimney Swifts
They billow out of a chimney.
Swirl, bank, hang, dive,
Tailing each other, crisscrossing,
Funneling back down the stack.

Fix your eyes on one,
Its sudden graceful swerves,
Cursive J, glissando,
Cryptography on cirrus.

        Cedar Waxwing
        Silk suit sophisticate,
        Admirable posture, shades,
        A scarlet pocket handkerchief.

        Or is that a wound,
        Pirate dandy, upside down
        Acrobat on the rigging?

Red-Winged Blackbirds
A legion swoops down on the reeds,
Epaulettes flashing. They sway
On the tips, they rattle and chime.
The sky over them opens.

Crows
The crows excoriate…what?
In the shadows and thick leaves.
Evermore. Evermore.
Evermore. Evermore.
Ad hoc choir of the disgruntled and tone deaf.
But they are heard.

Green Heron

(On dwelling in possibility)

1

A green heron flew out of the reeds and landed on a fallen tree where the Rondout Creek empties into the Hudson River. It paused, motionless, and became invisible. Had I not seen it fly in, I might never have seen it at all unless it moved. Occasionally, it did: first, a slow skulking down the limb, later a spreading of a wing like a cape over its head and down its side, like a magician whose exaggerated flourishes announce the drama about to unfold. But that comparison suggests a performance. The heron was not performing. Whether drying its wing, or shielding itself from the sun, it moved in secret. These were private, practical acts, not intended for my binoculars.

Meanwhile, near me, a fledgling tree swallow had

ventured to the tip of an oak branch that stretched over the water. It perched, bunched up and silent, until its parent swept over with food—insect remains from the mosquitoes, damsel flies, and sweat bees that populated the air just above the estuary waters. A squadron of tree and bank swallows dove and skimmed, and the fledgling was a beneficiary. When its parent approached, it fluffed up and squawked, as if to give her a bigger target. The parent remained airborne during each feeding, none of which lasted more than a second.

A second green heron emerged from a bank of cat-tails, and the contrast with the swallows' intensive hunting and feeding was striking. It showed no interest in the first heron. Stretching its long neck, it moved without refer-ence to the magician's display, though the two seemed to engage in tai chi, graceful and slow under the sun, not consciously linked to each other, let alone to the swal-lows' aerobatics or me.

A green heron isn't very green. You might be disap-pointed if you expect the cardinal or bluejay's Technicolor dreamcoat. His crest and back are opalescent, shading from dull grey to viridian, like the forest canopy when the sun hits it just right. What you'll likely notice first are the brown and white stripes of his belly that provide cam-ouflage among the reeds where he lurks. "Slinks," my wife Caroline said, "skulking about." She and my sons teased me for watching a YouTube video of a green heron, about eight minutes of amateur footage of one on a riverbank. There was no sinister plot, but "skulk" was the right word for the bird's movement. That I found this captivating has been a reference point any time I become self-righteous about what passes for entertainment among the young these days, or complain about the noisiness of modern movies or the shimmering nothingness of social media feeds. What could compare to that skulking green heron, they say, who isn't even green. Between DC and Marvel, we have Green Arrow and Green Lantern, Hawkeye and Falcon—birds and greenness, but no one thought to create a Green Heron. Any wonder?

Fair enough. Although his long beak could be a bayonet or lance, he's not otherwise superhero material. Then again, recall the monastic hero of the 1970s television series, *Kung Fu*. The show capitalized on the popularity of Bruce Lee films and a vogue for martial arts and, inexplicably, cast a white man of Irish descent, David Carradine, as a mixed-race Asian-American in the wild west. My elementary school friends and I were captivated by it. One scene in particular stands out; in fact, it's the only one that I recall. Kwai Chang Caine's master directs our hero to walk on rice paper without crinkling or tearing it. He fails repeatedly. Until he learns to quiet his body, the necessary poise and agility for expertise in martial arts won't follow. In third grade, we took butcher paper from the school supply closet and tried it ourselves. Why were bony redneck third graders drawn to an exercise of balletic grace? We imagined that skulking undetected was a prelude to an attack. Such agility would be combined with the speed and strength that allowed Bruce Lee to rip out a man's heart and show it to him before he died. I never saw this film scene, but others swore they had, and while we argued over whether the movie was real, no one doubted that a master of Lee or Caine's caliber could do it.

A heron slips along the shoreline as if on rice paper. A great angler, he will place a reflective object on the water's surface—a pin oak leaf, for example—and watch for a fish to investigate. The heron's patience, driven by necessity, far outstrips mine. Fifteen minutes in and I lower the binoculars to look for other birds. Meanwhile, the green heron waits, motionless, seemingly dispassionate, until a fish is in range and he strikes. Is it hyperbole to compare the jolt to lightning? His long neck shooting out and snapping back, he breaks the water's surface like a diver with barely a ripple and comes back with the catch. He is fed because he waited, quiet and watchful.

2

In its oldest forms, the English "wait" meant to lie

in wait upon, to spy or keep watch. Waiting was synonymous with watching—you didn't do one without the other—and the intent was suspicious. By the Middle Ages, the waiting became more about being observant and attentive than lying in wait. The OED cites the Wycliffe Bible version of Philippians 3:17, "Britheren, be ye my foleweris, and weyte ye hem that walken so, as ye han oure fourme," where the Vulgate Latin "observate" is rendered "weyte ye." Paul implores the early Christians to observe and imitate him and his followers as they have Jesus. It was around the late 1300s that "wait" also took on its most common contemporary meaning, to wait for, to remain in place until something happens. Depending on context, this waiting could be active or passive, anxious or meditative.

Waiting and watching eventually became separate actions. "Watch" became its own verb, even if "wait" still sometimes implied it. Today, we recombine them. In an early diagnosis of cancer, one is asked to begin "watchful waiting," a phase of patient attention to the tumor until it gives signs of needing treatment. As a concept, this watchful waiting seems to imply that it's common to do the opposite—to wait inattentively, to dawdle. Still, waiting involves anticipation, even if it's mild and no cause for anxiety—for the show to start, for instance, rather than for the cancer to require radiation.

To one who keeps time and makes lists, waiting seems wasteful, an undifferentiated space with no clear exit. To fill that space we invented the smartphone, a comfort object that gives the illusion of occupation or, worse, makes our occupation a constant companion. On the subway platform or the line at the deli, we scroll down our screens until we're poked or pinged or otherwise called on by friends or business, a surprisingly happy occasion that we respond to with overdetermined urgency, even if it means stumbling across the gap into the train or asking the cashier to hold on, annoying everyone behind us.

Before the phone, we had less captivating ways to occupy ourselves during the wait. The waiting room, modeled on purgatory, was cluttered with tattered issues of *People* and *Reader's Digest* and the prattle of afternoon talk shows. It was a poor distraction from what we anticipated. The wait's completion would be a dentist's chair or doctor's probes or the banker's tightening screws. The apparent wastefulness of biding our time was directly proportional to our resentment of being in that gray, unhappy limbo.

If it's possible to wait without watchfulness, it's impossible to do the opposite. Watching always involves waiting, but the watch can be so absorbing that time passes unnoticed. In the bird-watching community, nest cameras have become all the rage. Observing the preparation for a hatch, the hatch itself, the early feedings, and the fledging is like reading Book I of a long novel. That slow unfolding occupies us as fully as we will allow, since it is the details between events that constitute art just as they do living. If we're interested, the only thing that militates against our examining them closely is the time that we can commit. Watching a baseball game has a similar quality for enthusiasts. The poet George Oppen wrote that baseball is not a game but an argument, and few of us can tune out an argument before we know who won. It's the development that matters. The wait as such barely registers.

Watching should be distinguished from keeping watch, where one rewards absorption and the other requires alertness. The vigilance of keeping watch cannot be sustained indefinitely, and to endure the demands of the vigil, companionship helps. On the towers of Elsinore, Hamlet's friends could reassure each other of their sanity. "Yes, we saw a ghost," they could agree, "and it might be a sign."

For those who grew up with the Christmas story from the King James Bible or Handel's *Messiah*, "keep watch" likely calls to mind the language of the Gospel of Luke: "And there were in the same country shepherds abiding in the fields, keeping watch over their flocks by night." It's consistent with the gospel's radicalism, which has God's incarnation take place in a cattle stall, that the birth is announced first to people from the lowest social classes. And it's consistent with the gospel's symbology that they're shepherds, who, like the messiah they're about to encounter, watch over their flocks and intervene between them and danger. Finally, it's consistent with the King James translators' ear for poetry that in the rhythm of the sentence, a stress falls on "shepherds," then "abiding" and "keeping watch." Abidance and watchfulness are characteristic of Christianity, which began as an apocalyptic faith in a marginal community. Its followers kept watch and abided in each other's support.

In its earliest form in English, to abide meant to keep watch. The OED cites the West Saxon Gospel of Matthew 11:3. John the Baptist asks Jesus if he is the one for whom they have abided, where "abiden" signifies to wait and watch expectantly. Abide also always suggested dwell, and later translations of the Christmas story have the shepherds not abiding but dwelling, or less poetically (if more accurately) just "living," in the fields. The plenitude of a word like abide is a poet's field. My abode, my home, is a space of watchfulness. I dwell in anticipation, inside it, where I keep watch.

"Abide" also suggested "suffer" and "endure" early in its history. We dwell in bodies that suffer, and many of us abide in troubled places. Homes are often such places, and abiding the needs of others is necessary for

stability. Home is where we willingly endure another's sorrows and shortcomings. I might say "lovingly,"
because to abide means more than to put up with, just
as wait in its fullest sense includes the act of watching.
Homes, the primary spaces of our abidance, should be
inhabited by people who remain steadfast in concern
for each other. An old evangelical hymn petitions God,
"Abide with me"—wait with me, live with me, suffer my
flaws with sympathy—"fast flows the even tide." Because
we are time's subjects, because we recede at a pace that
we cannot foresee—unlike the tide, which is predictably
and thus more mercifully calibrated than our abidance on
this earth—we long for companionship. We want watch-
ers with us, a community in which to dwell.

3

To "dwell in possibility," as Emily Dickinson put it, is
a condition of wakefulness that shores against despair. It
requires presence and curiosity. It generates new thought,
which is new language. In this way, a walk by the river
resembles reading a poem. There is another life among
the reeds, and there are a hundred lives in the most
pedestrian of words. The urge to watch the heron sends
me down the winding path of etymology and lands me in
the pastoral idyll of a Wordsworth lyric despite the pings
of my phone.

> She dwelt among the untrodden ways
> Beside the springs of Dove,
> A Maid whom there were none to praise
> And very few to love

Wordsworth's "Maid"— this Lucy, whom so few knew—is the beauty in obscurity that poets of sensibility watched for and celebrated. A "violet by a mossy stone," her wonder, or rather the poet's wonder in her, derives in part from her loveliness being out-of-place and unexpected: she is a "violet by a mossy stone," an elegant heron among desiccated reeds. She dwelled "among the untrodden ways"—not "paths" or "places," but the more ambiguous "ways." A way is a gesture, this way or that way, a vague indication of a general direction. And it is a manner, a way of doing things or of being. But this is not the less traveled path that Frost would later claim, validating risk and independent thought. Lucy bided her time before the grave among unmapped spaces and customs that, Wordsworth implies, haven't brooked attention and may be the better for it.

It's not clear that Lucy knew she was being watched by the speaker, and we must impose on the lyric's empty spaces in order to imagine a relationship. What these untrodden ways seem to present to the "Maid" is an admirer who could never move closer, one who dwelt at a distance and chose to keep it that way. He loved the idyll, the snow globe pastoral by the Dove, and wouldn't disrupt it. When death cracks the glass, his surprise is as potent as it is pathetic. The pain he feels is captured in Wordsworth's brilliant, penultimate line: the flat, matter-of-fact "But she is in her grave" of monosyllables; the pause, indicated by the first comma, while words for the pain germinate; the conjunction "and," then another comma, as if to gasp the "oh" that follows; then yet another comma and a line break, the release of breath, the sigh:

> But she is in her grave, and, oh,
> The difference to me!

The "oh" also resuscitates a ballad filler (Oh, Susanna, don't you cry for me; what will you do for your daddy, oh), giving it semantic weight, in this case the speaker's sorrow and shock. We are compelled to stop and wait with him while he gathers words for his last line. That final exclamation turns the gaze inward, away from the idyll, for the "difference" proclaimed is in the speaker, who understands all that proceeded to have been of, even for, him. If we can forgive such narcissism (Keats called it Wordsworth's "egotistical sublime"), our forgiveness turns on our abidance. We linger long enough inside this lyrical ballad to appreciate the craft, which is its principal tribute to Lucy and what she represents. The untrodden way is the perfectly simple space of Wordsworth's small elegy, a space where we would notice a mossy stone and the violet nearby it, where we would reflect on the life of a passerby, and where we would pause to consider the pain of "oh" and the profundity of a comma.

4

One August Saturday, my brother and I kayaked the Davis Canal on Oak Island, NC. We drifted by a green heron, which Brian saw before I did, because he has always been more attuned to the details of the moment than I, even when I'm trying. The heron's stillness became ours—quiet but alert, attentive to the environment but not trapped in it, observant, connected. We watched until the current moved us too far and the heron faded into the shore. It was hard paddling back on course. But there was joy enough, more than enough, to sustain us.

Fruit

Nothing we planted produced.
Five cantaloupes volunteered in the compost.
All we did was water and admire them.
Cantaloupes are sweeter than I recall.

Looking Up

A woman crossing the street looked back over her shoulder at the sky above St. Joseph's Catholic Church. A jogger paused a few feet away and lifted his phone camera, while a man gesturing with his hands explained what was happening. It would be easy to miss what they saw, even if you are one who looks ahead instead of down at the sidewalk as I was when I stopped. It's rare that any of us look upward.

Monarch butterflies trickled by the bell tower: one // twothreefour //// five // sixseven / eight // nineten… Against the blue sky, one or a pair or a trio would materialize, fly over, and disappear again into the blue above the schoolhouse across the street. It was not breezy, but they were buffeted, as if navigating a restless sea on a raft. "Imagine that for 4500 miles," the woman exclaimed. "Glad I looked up."

I strode on to Half Moon Used Books, where I found a copy of Maggie Nelson's *Bluets* for the amount left on a giftcard I'd received at Christmas nine months earlier. Used bookshops affirm serendipity, and having teethed on the virtue of self-denial, I'm no good at just saying yes. Except that day, when I bought the book, and the owner, Jessica, and I joked about how well the paper giftcard had held up in my wallet. "Oh *Bluets*!" she said. "I loved that book. I hope you love it."

Nelson's last sentence is, "When I was alive, I aimed to be a student not of longing but of light."

On the walk home, I paused again at St. Joseph's and looked up at the monarchs. Onetwo // three //// four /// fivesixseven // tossed around but not turning off. The ones who come back next spring will be the great grandchildren. I watched the bell tower until the stream dried up.

And then there was a Luna moth in the parking lot of the school. I'm not imagining this for effect, though no one was there with me to witness. It sailed by as I set out again, green after orange, yes after yes.

It Suggests to Our Faith

A Brief History of the Silver Melon Project

The discovery was made, as with so many great archaeological finds, by someone who wasn't searching, in a place that hundreds, maybe thousands, of people had been. Although descending to the ice cave required skill, many had crossed right over the crevasse where on a July afternoon a twenty-two year old woman visiting from Singapore paused to adjust her headlamp and was momentarily blinded by the glint of her light off a metallic object many feet below. Photos that she and her partner posted from their phones initiated the curiosity seekers and ultimately the dig that closed the cave and led to the extraction of a metallic capsule. Weighing approximately 100 pounds, it resembled a watermelon and earned the nickname "silver melon" from the excavators.

Based on the age of the rock and the position of the vessel deep in the crevasse, geologists concluded—to the surprise of the scientific community and the joy of UFO seekers—that it had arrived before the last glacier scraped across what is now the American northeast. The silver melon was a vessel from another world, but engineers could not decipher how it flew or landed. Cleaned and fully restored, it had no visible means of propulsion. There were no seams in the shell, and it was only with the aid of electron microscopy that inscriptions were discovered: thousands of lines of what appeared to be verse, encircling the melon from tip to tip.

"For this we had no Rosetta Stone," confessed Dr. Joseph Tonsgaard, linguist in charge of the team that deciphered the verse. Three years into the research, the team announced that the inscription contained features of the characters of the earliest forms of all known world languages. Although the semantics of the verse were still incomprehensible, the team hypothesized that this object from elsewhere would alter our understanding of the source and evolution of language itself.

That hypothesis acquired a wide following on the evening that the vessel began to emit sounds. Having determined that the initial series of characters at one end of the ship (subsequently designated the "fore") might be translated, "into [or toward] the daylight [or sun]," it was proposed that the silver melon be brought into the sunlight. The proposal is said to have originated with a

Ms. An Jiang, a promising graduate assistant from Nepal. It was hotly contested for several days by senior archaeologists and material scientists, who maintained that re-exposure to the elements could cause unforeseeable, irreparable damage. Engineers were confident that the melon entered the atmosphere in a casing that has since been lost, or that burned up in the vessel's descent. A compromise was reached when the advocates of exposure agreed to postpone the sun ceremony until the surface had been fully replicated in an actual-size model of the melon, in steel of the exact quality of the original.

On the late afternoon of 21 July 20--, the silver melon was wheeled onto the roof garden of the Roosevelt laboratory, "among the petunia planters," recalled Professor Stepan Ahkmatov, who was appointed lead researcher of the Silver Melon Project. "It couldn't have occurred to any of us to invite a musicologist," he admitted, but because the event was filmed not only officially but also by numerous phones, there are multiple versions of the melon's first sounds. "Like a lute and voice," Mr. Sean O'Hara remarked. Mr. O'Hara was a member of the security detail and a self-described fan of early music.

The sounds have since been determined to resemble most closely the dutar of Central Asia, interfused with plainchant, as if performed in a cathedral. Although the meaning of this mysterious evensong, initiated by the declining sun, awaited further effort from the linguists, the effect was immediate and astonishing. All flora and fauna within its acoustic range responded. Flowers bent toward the source, leaves pivoted in its direction. Insects paused: beetles seemed to freeze, dragonflies and moths to hover. As for people, a variety of sensations were reported. Common to all was a tingling felt across the entire surface of the body. Most people described a comparable sensation inside their bodies, as if their bones and organs were responding. "One sensed that one understood something," Dr. Ahkmatov explained.

The music also opened a small portal on starboard.

The portal was not detected until the following day when the surface was being re-scanned by electron microscopy to check for damage from the exposure to sunlight. It was a special character—only one was found on the entire vessel. Linguists speculated that it was a proper name. In context, it seems to represent a place. "A sacred point of origin," according to Dr. Tonsgaard, "or perhaps a holy destination." It was determined that the opening—a kind of portal—was protected by a transparent substance with tensile strength equal to the surrounding steel. The portal was recessed, allowing for partial penetration into the vessel.

Peering through the portal required the construction of a robotic periscope, "the weight and diameter of an infant's hair," said Professor Eleanora Liptak, a materials engineer who chaired the design team. Such delicate, complex work takes time and considerable expense. Funding was provided by the government of Canada, which named the completed periscope "Nakuset," the sun of the Mi'kmaq people. Prof. Liptak hails from the Maritime Provinces.

Capable of infrared videography, sonar, and heat detection, Nakuset mapped a wedge of the melon visible from the portal. Extrapolating from the wedge map, scientists described the interior as a dense network of compartments, layered and stacked like a honeycomb and held at a constant temperature of zero centigrade. The temperature is not affected by changes outside the vessel. "If we learn nothing more from all this research than how the melon is insulated, we will improve the lives of millions," said Ambassador Peter Ngozi of the United Nations commission charged with international over-sight of the research and findings.

Each compartment appeared to have contents of the same shape and mass. Some five years into the research, close inspection of multiple stills from the video yielded the first strong evidence to support the popular specula-tion that the silver melon was a mausoleum. Whether the cells contained bodies was not clear. Translations of the initial verses, which began to be published in those same weeks, offered clues.

Teams of linguists devised three competing translations of the text. None could claim to be definitive; all were equally plausible. Here is a composite, with variants:

> Into [toward] the daylight [sun] commend
> these vessels [containers, bodies]
> They the million [multitude], them the gardeners [planters, sowers]

The second line serves as a refrain that recurs 48 times, each as the second line in what researchers concluded were stanzas in a base six form. Although the words are inscribed continuously in concentric circles around the surface, the opening is a poem of 48 stanzas and 288 six-word lines that concludes with the mysterious character on the starboard portal. Scholars believe that the music is a performance of the poem, an invocation of a deity and a declaration of the mission of the capsule. The verses and remaining inscriptions—thousands of lines altogether—are still being translated and interpreted.

The preponderance of evidence at that stage of the research favored the theory that the capsule was filled with "seeds" intended to promote the spread of a civilization and its ideas. Whether these seeds were actual biological organisms that would germinate under the right conditions, or inorganic objects meant to influence ideas and creativity, or whether the cells might contain more, such as the remains of alien bodies or records from an extraterrestrial civilization—all, or a combination, seemed plausible. Definitive conclusions would be elusive until the capsule's entrance could be discovered or the capsule cut open.

The most aggressive researchers advocated the latter. They were supported by a majority of the UN commission. "The international community has an interest in fully understanding this message from another world," said Ambassador Ngozi. "As long as it could be opened safely, the commission sees no reason to delay." Safety, however, was a significant concern. "We were worried not only about disturbing the contents," explained Dr. Ahkmatov, "but also about what might be activated or released, especially if the vessel was improperly penetrated." To the layperson, such concerns recalled superstitions about disturbing the sarcophagi of Egyptian mummies, but scientists warned of the potential presence of pathogens or the detonation of an explosion intended to deter just such an invasion. Before any opening of the capsule, the most secure conditions would need to be created.

The silver melon was removed to a weapons testing facility in an undisclosed location believed to be underground in the desert southwest of the United States. The research team's engineers devised a robotic laser and pincer as a component of Nakuset. Inside a sealed chamber, the glass of the portal would be slowly cut and removed. Nakuset's periscope would be inserted further into the capsule to videorecord a wider sample of the interior. From this recording, decisions could be made about what to remove for closer inspection and testing.

But on the evening before the procedure, the capsule opened.

At 12:00 the second-shift watch received an alert of a disturbance in the sealed chamber. "The screens suddenly lit up," Lance Corporal Dominique Garret recalled, "and faster than I could signal the team, things started happening."

The metallic shell of the capsule unfurled in thin layers, slowly and smoothly, as if the shell were liquefying and spreading across the room. This became a canvas onto which the cells of the honeycomb dispersed, millions of them, like dandelion seeds, but all seemingly directed to a predetermined spot. The contents of each cell burst into color and light, all as the music of the capsule caused the thick glass and walls of the sealed room to vibrate. After the unfolding ended, the silver melon had transformed into an intricate atlas of all life and events on the earth from the moment of the capsule's arrival to the present. Every perspective, every surface of the globe, occupied by humans or not; every minute of time from that evening of the landing to the moment just past; seemed to have been mapped. "If one believed in a god who sees every sparrow that falls," said Professor Ahkmatov, "this would be her memory."

Those memories played continuously but not chronologically, and researchers had no means of pausing, skipping, or selecting. For the first week, a random assortment of brief holograms, scenes so vivid that witnesses described odors, temperature, and the heft of bodies in space, skipped across history and represented every continent. The first detailed holograms, which lasted three days, simultaneously displayed the hunting of an auroch by Khiamian peoples near the Dead Sea, the births of two children in a women's prison in Louisiana in 1973, and the funeral and interment of the remains of a Russian soldier after the Battle of Borodino in 1812. "We do not know how the three were connected, or if they were," Professor Ahkmatov admitted. "We scrambled to bring in the right historians and anthropologists before the projections changed." By the fourth day, when the second projection began—a single, five-day panorama of life in an Incan village that included everything from the quotidian ablutions of the king's consorts to the conversation among the enslaved as they cultivated maize—a heated international debate had ensued over making the projections public by streaming them online. Having millions of minds concentrated on this detailed review of time would increase the opportunity for learning and would assist in the revision and expansion of the historical and scientific record. But to grant open access might be to ignore potential harm.

At the time of this writing, the atlas has not displayed anything controversial. It has not, for instance, entered the closed executive session of a Fortune 500 company, let alone the bedroom of a living couple. It has not displayed incontrovertible evidence that an executed inmate was innocent and that the guilty party lived to celebrate the birth of a grandchild. It has not replayed My Lai or the latest conversation between the US president and her secretary of state. "We have to assume that until the controls are discovered," Ambassador Ngozi argued, "such controversial, potentially explosive memories could be projected at any point." So access currently remains restricted to the original team of scientists and scholars and a delegation from the UN Commission, who determine what projections may be disseminated.

The final cell on the map—in the bottom, right corner—is the portal. Some now wonder whether it is not only a window but also a lens, and if it is a lens, whether it is an eye or a projector. If we are watching the memory of God, are we being watched and recorded? Or might we ourselves be the projections of God's forethought? The projections could be the record of our being observed by another civilization, up to the present: the silver melon is an indiscriminate recorder. Or they could be the story that the capsule always contained and that we lived into existence: the silver melon seeded human history. There is some hope that fully deciphering the inscriptions will provide further clues. The portal still appears to be open, despite lying flat in the corner of the atlas. But researchers can no longer see into it. If they could—when they learn how to do so—we may discover the other side of the atlas: the mind's eye of our observers, or the predetermined stories of our tomorrows.

Late Autumn, Hiding

1

From the brush pile
A blast of blue jays
Clears the air.

2

Nine robins in the bittersweet
It's November, they're leaving.
The neighbor's child practices oboe.

3

A field cricket chirps
Unanswered, persistent.
Snow came early.

Red-Necked Grebe

It had flown already.
I had dropped everything
To go see it.

Three scaups scooted
Among the dwindling ice floes
On the Hudson.

Group-home boys
Balanced on the defunct trolley rails
And pushed each other over.

A cocker spaniel
In a sweater like a tea cozy
Was named Brady.

The 3:15 Amtrak to New York
Glimmered down the opposite bank,
Bright under bare trees.

I will misquote the Apostle Paul:

"Whatever is true and pleasing,
If there is anything worthy of praise,
Think about these things."

Don't get me wrong:
I would like to see a red-necked grebe,
Another one, on a different day.

Still on the walk home
Toddlers in pink and orange parkas
Ran ahead of their mothers,

Paused,
And ran back,
Laughing.

Paradise Lost

Those few souls brought back from the dead,
Wings shorn, newfound understanding blurred,
What must they have thought of their return?

Light crackles in the fog like fireflies
And they're back in it, stunned,
Joyful maybe, anxious surely.

"Now will I lose my life again?"
Lazarus demanded of his sisters
While he slathered bread with honey.

What effort to readjust a body,
To coax slow hands and dim eyes,
To succumb once more to limits,

Though after the coma the jazz pianist discovered
His right and left hands had independent minds,
And his soul crouched close to the surface.

Still they must wonder, "Why me?
Why not Emmett Till, or Jacqueline Du Pré?
Why not the Sandy Hook children?"

What's the use of such questions, such guilt or fear?
Give sweets to the mouth, let fingers roam,
Find everyone you hurt and kiss them.

"Easy enough for you to say," they reply,
"With your one life, one death,
Fledged from some future forked branch."

Cormorant in the Tree of Life

Late autumn beech tree
Bronzed when the rest are bare
On the peninsula in the estuary.

Midmorning November sun
Rakes away the damp
Of the world and your outspread wings.

Ragged black against gold,
Serpentine neck, acned cheek,
Belch rattles up from your belly,

Insisting on paradise.

Hurt Crow

Untroubled by your trouble
you chortle at the coyote.
Under wing, night falls.
"The fire god is here
to look for fire."

"Photos too bad to display
but too good to throw out"

Was how we labeled the box.
We were moving again.
The landlord laughed when he read it,
"Like some relatives."
Many were duplicates ("two prints
for the price of one")
but we kept both, the way a church
keeps every Bible,
or a school every flag,
things that won't become garbage
without crying shame on you
in their humiliation and redundancy.
      Our youngest son rescued stuffed animals
from curbside heaps. The one-eyed koala
brought us bedbugs as well as joy
but when his eye pleaded, who could leave him
with chicken parts and Kleenex,
destined for the city dump?
He's in the attic with the box
of photos too bad to display.
      Every attic borders a landfill
as cemeteries border emptiness.
Two generations go by then the tombstones,

like attic bric-a-brac, accuse us:
"You should know what I meant.
They promised not to forget."
Not forgetting evaporates.
It becomes the clarity of not remembering.
Leave your attic to a grandchlld.
He'll know what to do with that
box of photos too bad to display
but too good to throw out.
      I searched ours yesterday,
two decades after we labeled it. I wanted
a picture to fill the gap, the year between events,
no graduation or wedding or births,
days that we must have had our coffee and tea,
left for and returned from work,
walked the dog, read together in bed,
all too ordinary to remember but
didn't we snap one lousy photo?
      Now the children snap everything,
flattening out the memorable, or maybe
appreciating the quotidian,
recording it, displaying it with too little forethought.
Still I say save it, especially what seems boring.
You will need to fill gaps.
Ask a trusted neighbor to snap
you and your partner unawares as you

return from walking your wiener dog in light rain
when you are holding hands, your hair disheveled,
cloth sneakers damp, but you are smiling.
Or when you're someday weeding the flowerbeds
as neighborhood kids pedal down the walks
and house sparrows dustbathe.
Or even when you sit on the steps
with your head in your hands and the dog
rests her snout on your feet.
      Mind the gap, the London Tube warns.
It widens, if you're fortunate to live long enough.
It becomes the life, full in its normality,
colorful in emptiness,
everything worth saving in a big enough box.

The Meadow

Crossing a meadow with no horizon
I came upon a man in a wooden chair
That needed to be re-caned. He perched
On the back with a bucket between his knees.
"For rain water?" I asked, and he nodded.
"Sometimes a goldfinch visits and sips."
Grass had just begun to break the sod.
"Am I walking in the right direction?"
He removed his straw hat and waved,
Ran his hand across his baldness,
Stroked his long beard.
"Everyone asks that," he said,
"Spring has arrived, there will be
More light, and fragrance."
He replaced his hat and offered water
From a tin ladle on the bucket.
I had not known how thirsty I was.
I worried about taking too much.
He assured me that it would rain
Soon enough, even pour down,
"A barrel would be too small."
"What about shelter?" I asked,
Seeing no trees or cliffs, only meadow.
"You're wearing a cap," he noted,

"And that overcoat should shed water.
Tuck your shoes under your arm
And don't put them on again till
Your feet dry." I thanked him
For his advice.
                    Further on
Clouds gathered, flocks of finches,
Dozens, then hundreds, descended
Gold and purple on the meadow.
To my surprise, they were silent.
I held out my cap, and one flew in,
A house finch, missing an eye.
"What happened?" I thought.
She must have read my face.
"Hailstone, when we crossed the gulf.
Don't be concerned! The benefit
Of a flock is we guide each other."
She preened while she spoke—or
Sang, her speech was melodic,
Like a recitative, and confident.
"How far to the meadow's edge?
You must have crossed it in flight."
She ignored my question.
"In time you will come to a pecan tree.
The ground is covered with nuts
No one harvested. Fill your cap and pockets."

I scanned the meadow but saw no tree.
"Dare I ask how far?" I dared ask.
My finch hovered by my ear, "Would you
Walk faster or slower if you knew?"
Lifting all at once, the flocks caused a breeze
That raked across the tiny meadow grasses.
It smelled of cinnamon.
I cannot say how long I walked. Night
Came and went and came again, rain
Fell and slaked my thirst, I slept
While walking as if in a dream
Until the tree was before me.
In its broad shade, I lay
Against the trunk and cracked
Pecans in my palms. The meadow stretched
Endless around me, north, south, east, west.
"Is this all?" I wondered aloud.
A breeze rattled the branches in bud.
I foresaw the catkins and new fruit,
A downpour under ten thousand leaves,
Their slow shedding of green for gold,
A fire in winter kindled from windfall,
And the grass soughed, "Sufficient for you."

Bowl of Rice, Bottle of Nard

As our family dog, Gabby, grew old, we learned that an aging pet becomes a new creature. Her behavior and language changes, but she expects you to understand. Gabby needed us to translate and accommodate. First came the constant low-level anxiety. She cried for our attention but was often, to our dismay, inconsolable. This began in the Covid-19 summer not long after, coincidentally, fireworks were legalized in New York. So for all of July we attributed Gabby's torment to the incessant cherry bombs and whistlers fired by stir crazy teens in Covid-19 isolation. Holding her, wrapping her tight in a blanket, moving into confined spaces—these offered temporary reprieve, but nothing cured the trembling and terror. Then came the food obsession and thirst, and our suspicion was belatedly roused. Gabby had never begged for food, and her constant need of water was easy enough to diagnose as kidney failure.

In the months that followed, our goals were to prevent discomfort and enable her to continue to experience joy and love with as little medical intervention as possible. There were CBD treats and changes of diet, which provided modest relief. There was getting up in the night as when we had infant children. Eventually she began to wander into corners, to seem disoriented and unsure, but when we would go to her and look in her eyes, there would still be a light. When she stopped drinking, we decided to administer fluids subcutaneously. That in itself moved us toward a level of medical intervention that we thought we would avoid. But when the vet's treatment gave her almost a week of renewed strength and tail wagging, we asked to be trained.

I have been averse to needles my whole life. The first time I gave blood, as a high school senior, I turned green and fainted in front of my would-be girlfriend. Things never improved. When Caroline required a spinal tap to relax enough to give birth to our first son, it was I who ended up flat on my back with my feet above my head. They gave me orange juice while Caroline got the pain meds. I was not our top choice for injecting Gabby. But on the day that we could get the training from the vet, I was the one available. I watched closely as the vet techs demonstrated the steps: take the cap off the needle; make a tent of skin at the scruff of Gabby's neck; insert the needle just under the skin ("If it pokes through, don't worry! That happens! Just try again!"); flip the release valve on the tubing; elevate the bag and squeeze it to speed the flow; at 100 ml, close the valve and remove the needle; dispose of the needle in a sharps container ("We'll provide one!"); replace with a new capped needle for next time.

I did not faint. I didn't even become queasy. When I later performed the procedure with Caroline and Sammy observing, I was equally unaffected. Why? It can only be that when necessity demanded it, I could focus on the procedure as such. Gabby would benefit, the method could be learned, I could learn it. Do the task, and be careful to do it correctly. Although remarkable for my lack of fainting, there is nothing praiseworthy about my performance. Caregivers daily perform much more emotionally demanding and complex medical tasks. For over a decade, my mother gave insulin shots to my grandmother twice per day. She rotated the site of the shot to minimize long-term bruising: left arm, left hip, right arm, right hip. She dressed an open skin cancer wound on my grandmother's temple. Dispassionate, methodical, and attentive: such is loving care of the sick body of the beloved.

In the Sāmannaphala Sutta, there is a story about the centrality of caring for others on the path to awakening. King Ajatasattu questions the Buddha about the fruits of the ascetic life. It's clear, he suggests, how the monk benefits from withdrawing into the sangha, letting go of possessions, and devoting himself to mindfulness, his physical needs supplied by those who continue to labor in the world. But how does monasticism benefit everyone else, he asks? Put less politely, Ajatasattu's question would be, "what good is a monk?" or, "how is a monk any different from a moocher?" The Buddha replies that the monks' dependency inspires others to care for them. In this, they provide as great a lesson as their teaching of the scriptures. In ascertaining someone else's needs and then finding the means to satisfy them, we practice not thinking about ourselves, and selflessness moves us closer to the awakened state of non-self.

There is a similar moment in the Christian gospels. When Jesus visits Mary and Martha in Bethany, Mary washes his feet with perfume and dries them with her hair. Judas, the apostles' bookkeeper and eventually the betrayer, casts aspersions on the extravagance of this act, because her bottle of nard could have been sold and the proceeds given to the poor. Jesus responds without denying the truth of Judas' objection but by encouraging a different perspective on Mary's extravagance. The poor are always with you, he says, but I am with you for a short time. Homeless, ascetic, and a gifted teacher, Jesus was a singular case whose presence encouraged acts of extravagant hospitality, in part because he was devoted to the poor and outcast.

134

It's possible to have it both ways: to take care of everyone, and be indulgent to your beloved. Scale and resources are less often the problem than will. There is a routineness to caregiving. Bathe the wound twice daily with iodine. There are radical acts of beneficence. Cut off and sell your hair to buy your lover a platinum watch chain. Both are necessary.

Down by the river in late April, the swallows were back—barn, tree, and rough-winged, all in a mixed flock.

The plainness of this statement belies the joy I felt in watching them. Returning from their winter elsewhere, they turned somersaults over the estuary. Imagine if they left colored contrails. The early evening air would be a Spirograph page. Maybe you're too young to remember that pen-and-paper toy. Think multi-colored polygons and overlapping lattices.

Chimney sweeps returned shortly and resumed their evening shows. Right now, one of our neighbors sits on his porch and coughs the seismic, rib-cracking cough of emphysema. His cough is familiar in the neighborhood, otherwise I would suspect Covid-19. It comes again and again, waning when he quits cigarettes for a while, returning with force when he resumes. The sweeps natter above while he snatches at air.

Among the many American shortcomings laid bare

by the pandemic, this was the greatest: that we value individual liberty over the common good. The simplest gesture of care for others was to wear a mask. Everyone might have done it voluntarily out of respect for their neighbor's wellbeing, but since altruism was in short supply, governments intervened. What outrage followed such an intolerable imposition of state control! I need only write, "Michigan." The former President mocked his compliant opponent and held super-spreader events even after he became sick. State governments outlawed mask mandates after the vaccine was available, even as schools reopened and the majority of their residents refused vaccines. An American may choose to help, but he cannot be required to do so, especially not if the requirement appears to compromise his liberty to resist and go his own way.

As a young Southern Baptist in the 1970s, I was taught to pray for forgiveness of my "sins and shortcomings." The distinction was never explained to me, but I always assumed that it came from a passage in Paul's letter to the Romans, "For all have sinned, and come short of the glory of God." Protestants, especially the fundamentalist sort, do not parse sin into categories or hell into tiers. There never has been nor will be a Protestant Purgatory beyond life itself. Still, even the evangelical believer with the purest heart, the one who genuinely seeks not to covet or kill or commit lustful thoughts, let alone acts, even that person will fall short through negligence, or ignorance, or weak effort. In my skeptical moments, which were sinful by that definition, I wondered how natural weakness or innate incapacity, or even just bad luck that impeded full blossoming or exuberant engagement, could be held against someone in the same way as adultery or homicide. But in my experience, conservative Christians did not suffer the devil to tempt them with visions of grey areas or border cases. Even if you were dealt a weak hand, it was still up to you to beat the odds.

Americans are obsessed with measuring up. The other side of individual liberty is individual accountability. To fall short of expectations may be the cardinal American sin. Consider the fact that in the name of educational progress, liberals and conservatives alike set about reforming public education in the 90s and early 00's by establishing academic standards and instituting tests to detect whether every child met them. Because Americans tend to believe that the marketplace offers the most powerful incentives for innovation and the most potent correctives of shortcomings, reform required competition—among schools, within buildings, between kids. Borrowed from business, the language of "quality assurance" and "continuous improvement" became eduspeak, too. If a school met the standards in some areas, but not in others, the tests would highlight the shortcoming, and an improvement plan would be put in place.

When the scores came back and decisions were made, no child was unaware of the fact when he was the one who failed. He fell short. It's he who had to undergo the intervention and be re-tested. It was he (often male, often from poverty) whose shortcoming was…what, exactly? Not being a quick enough learner, a serious enough student, a savvy enough test-taker? Or was there a character flaw? The unintended consequence of American exceptionalism is that everyone comes up short at some point, but a predictable subset comes to be defined by their supposed shortcomings.

To think in terms of shortcomings is to focus on flaws rather than potential. Our care for others in the pandemic fell far short of what was needed or desirable; generously, we could account it a shortcoming that points to an American character flaw. But like our obsession with the putative educational shortcomings of our children, it may be more accurately described as a sin of commission—a crime knowingly committed, one that harmed many in the interest of a few. Whether a sin or a shortcoming, America's response to the needs of others during the pandemic left us with a debt that we cannot repay. Too many died.

Owing a debt, you "come short" or "fall short" when you count your last pennies in front of the creditor. "To come short of" and its twin, "to fall short of," became commercial language very early in the history of the two phrases. The abbreviated "shortfall" was a much later, Gilded Age term, but it was shorthand for the already well-established phrase. Accountability in finances, academics, and matters of the soul shouldn't use the same ledger and arbiter. But in time, any series of transactions will find one party falling short of the other. If we're to balance the two sides, mercy will be required.

Reflect on Paul's claim that everyone "comes short of the glory of God." Paul's version of God can be distilled in the word "caritas," a love that is expressed in care. Our aim should be to care for the earth and our fellow creatures as if we were beings defined by caritas. We will fall short even when we try, because our capacity to care is limited by our own needs and desires. The self is an impediment. But forgiving our shortcomings, others will follow our model and step in. What good is a monk? We can work together to take care of him. If I come up short, you will step in, and vice-versa.

Our shortcomings with fellow humans during the pandemic were egregious. But even at the best of times, we behave in ways that assume that nonhuman animals, their habitats and bodies, belong to us and should be subject to our interests. Setting aside the numerous wild animals in our midst, even in urban areas, that we displace, pollute, run over, and poison, our assumption that any human interest takes precedence over the nonhuman is true even of the animals we purport to care for—the animals that depend on us. The roots of "depend" in Latin communicate an essential aspect of the relationship, for in its earlier uses, "depend" suggested to hang from or upon. Our animals are connected to us—sometimes literally by a leash, but always for their wellbeing. "Our" should suggest not ownership but responsibility, as it does in "our children" or "our aging parents."

It never seemed correct to refer to myself as Gabby's "owner." In my (admittedly sentimental) household, we tend to use family language—Gabby's mum, her brothers. That, too, is incorrect, but it errs on the side of a caring relationship, in which we depend on each other. It emphasizes the bond. Today when we say, "that depends," we acknowledge contingency in a way that is distantly connected to the word's etymology. "Should I feed the dog?" That depends on whether she's already been fed, not on whether you're in the mood or feel it's someone else's duty. Her needs are dependent. Even if the dependency is not visible, we are aware of it. That feeling of urgency, of needing to do something for the feral cat or stray dog, to take them in, also points to how much we depend on our dependents. We are almost as much theirs as they are ours, because the act of caring satisfies a need that is as basic as hunger.

It is easy enough to accept all of this in reference to pets, but it should extend, at the very least, to all domesticated animals—for instance, the cows, chickens, pigs, and other creatures that people cultivate for food. Animal rights activists have pushed for humane treatment of animals grown for food and have drawn attention to the inhumanity of factory farms. Gentler interactions between farmhands and livestock put the creatures at ease and lead to fewer injuries among workers. Gates and chutes that account for the creature's perspective have the same mutual benefits. But as the philosopher Steve Cooke argues, all of these efforts in effect cause the nonhuman animal to trust the human. This is pernicious, for what is the endgame if not a betrayal of the trust? Humane slaughter is an oxymoron and rationalization. No nonhuman animal seeks its death; the only example of a humane imposition of death on a fellow creature is euthanasia to alleviate its suffering, and even that decision should be approached with humility and reverence.

After having worked on farms throughout my childhood, I became vegetarian 25 years ago. The turning point for me was a *Washington Post* exposé on factory farms in Virginia. I had been inside massive turkey barns, debeaking chicks and picking up dead. I had never thought of the process of farming poultry as inhumane, let alone immoral, because I had not thought of farm animals as fellow creatures. I take that term, "fellow creatures," from Christine Korsgaard, whose book by that title states my position on the matter with greater philosophical clarity than I can. Put simply, many species—many more than we generally wish to acknowledge—are not merely sentient but also have the capacity to desire things and seek them out. In a sense, they set goals and work toward them. These may be immediate and simple, but they are substantive from the creature's point of view, and they are the basis of its moral status. On what grounds, therefore, do we justify removing the creature's capacity to pursue its ends? That is, how can we justify caging it, let alone killing it?

Ignoring animal suffering is a shortcoming shared by millions who have the privilege to know better and alleviate it, if just a little. Long before I read the animal liberation and ethics literature, I became vegetarian because I made myself confront the self-evident fact that I could survive without eating animals. Is it not better to assume that all of our fellow creatures prefer to remain alive? If my context was different—if food was scarce, for example, or my family's survival depended on eating animals—the calculus might change, but for a healthy, employed adult in middle class America, it is impossible to argue that meat is a necessity. I admit that my argument is too simple to be consistent. I don't eat meat because I do not want animals to die for my food. But I lament that I am falling short: even on free range, organic farms, dairy and egg production remain connected to the meat industry. I have not yet succeeded in veganism, though doing so would be logically consistent with my position about the moral status of our fellow creatures.

Caring for aging pets leads to decisions about not only alleviating but also ending their suffering. In the span of two weeks during the second spring of the pandemic, Gabby and our pet rabbit, Tim, became so ill that we made the decision for euthanasia. Both had lived long for their species. As a middle school child eight years earlier, our son Jacob brought Tim home unannounced. A frail bunny, Tim required hand feeding and constant care, which Caroline provided, so he became her rabbit, bonded to her, but also generally amiable to all creatures. Gabby came to us as a puppy rescued from a mill. She had been good-natured as well, especially toward children. A dachshund and Jack Russell hybrid, light on her white paws, she walked all over our hometown of Kingston with us: daily to elementary school and back with the boys when they were little, often to the church where we volunteered. People recognized her. She raised their spirits.

A dear friend—a Greek immigrant, a person of faith, intellect, and curiosity who, in her aging, has grown wise about the challenges we face as the body slows down—sighed from her depths, "Pets are our history." I scrolled through family photos, and Gabby was in more than half of them: lying on the couch by Caroline as she read to the boys, looking up at Jacob in a candid of him talking to his friends, nosing among the wrappings on Christmas morning. Her presence at every notable event implies that she was always around, that she was present in the quotidian routines that we barely recall but that are most of the content of life. I use the term "present" advisedly. She was there more fully than some of the people. She was not simply on the timeline, but was the steadiness of time itself.

Gabby was the first pet we raised as a young family. When Caroline and I met many years before, I had a dachshund named Wagner. Caroline claims that he was part of the attraction, and they bonded on the first occasion, when she walked back to my place after class, I gave her soup (another attraction, she claims), and the two chased each other around that dank, Virginia basement apartment. Prone to seizures, Wagner was an anxious dog, his anxiety probably exacerbated by my own, which I medicated in those days with too much whiskey and beer. Caroline brought the virtue of calm attentiveness, and he became a happier dog when she entered our lives. That history—our meeting, becoming a couple, marrying…in essence, our growing up—was Wagner's, too. When the boys were born, however, we lost focus on him. Did we miss the cancer because we were so distracted by babies and work? By the time we realized that he was ill, it was too late to intervene.

We are told that it is a mercy to end a suffering animal's life. I had to trust this during those two spring weeks. For both Gabby and Tim, the suffering was not otherwise going to cease, and that clarity made the decision possible. Nonetheless, to have signed off on the death of a fellow creature kept me awake for several nights. I found it hard to breathe. Sorrow can feel too much like guilt—the same heaviness and hollowness, the same disorientation and fatigue. Should we have given them another day? It's rare that nature "takes its course" and spares us these decisions.

Caroline held Tim after the vet administered the barbiturate. "Did he seem comforted?" she asked me several times in the days that followed. "It's important to me that he was comforted." I had the same wish with Gabby: that as life left her, what I saw in her eyes was her knowledge of our love. Often we lament that animals cannot speak to us, that they don't have language, at least not one with the variety and complexity of human speech. But they teach us how to listen to them. We must pay attention consistently, over long stretches of time, to learn what our fellow creatures are communicating through gesture, movement, and sound, or simply through their eyes. It's a gift they offer us, like their constancy, a bowl of rice, and their enthusiasm when we return, a bottle of nard.

Creekbank Imaginary

("The Cuckoo," Roud 413)

The cuckoo, she's a pretty bird
She warbles as she flies
She never says cuckoo
Till the fourth day of July.

The clock that hung on a nail on the front porch was a pine cottage with gingerbread along the eaves and hands painted green like loblolly needles. Two red doors snapped open to let the bird out. They were reliable, but the bird sometimes caught on a hinge. If no one was around to assist, she cuckooed inside her cave, accompanied by the angry clicks and clatters of her gears. Then the doors snapped shut.

Under the clock is the banjo player. When he sings, the banjo keeps an unsteady rhythm—one and two and;

one and two and three; one and two; one and two and—as if his hands made one melody, his voice another, all in a minor key, driving forward and unsettled. "That's how it goes," he laughs.

His wife rocks on a stool and keeps unsteady time. She smiles, her few teeth burnished with snuff. Cataracts veil her eyes. She sees in cloud formations. A heavy mist has rolled up from the creek and blanketed the porch, eliminating her disadvantage.

There is a third person. He sits on an overturned bucket. Bareback and bare legged, he is the only one who is dressed for the heat. He has made a table from two other buckets and a plank. He is cleaning suckers, pitching their heads and entrails to a hoard of cats. He favors a quiet, orange one that sits in the corner behind the woman. On a tine of his trident gig, he reaches it a filleted chunk. When the others slink over, he smacks them with the pole.

No one wants to heat the cabin further in the summer swelter, so in the yard a grill is warming, its coals glowing through the fog. A swill of lard in a cast iron pan has just begun to simmer. Nearby in the woods, cuckoos have started calling.

The calls sound nothing like the clock's cuckoo. Do you remember Mutual of Omaha's *Wild Kingdom*, the episodes on an ice sheet crowded with elephant seals? Their trumpeting and the bird's call are in the same section of the orchestra—the reedy tones of an English horn and bassoon. As for the cuckoo's song, it is neither a warble nor the cheery piping of the clock bird. Think of laser guns in an arcade game of the 1980s. The yellow-billed cuckoo, the species in the pine forest around the cabin, is a space invader.

In sound, that is, because this space belongs to no one, all boundaries and claims and deeds being temporary impositions, the conversion of space to place. The woods are like the ballad, a palimpsest. Long before the cabin, when an earlier variant of "The Cuckoo Bird" was sung in a major key in the English countryside about a bird of another species, this clearing by the creek was Chickasaw, and the yellow-billed cuckoo's call and song…what might they have been compared to? How might they have been imitated, and what would a fine imitation sound like?

The cuckoo, she's a pretty bird

She warbles as she flies

She bring us good tidings

She tells us no lies

The banjo player's wife, Esther, rises and walks slowly, guided by sound, routine, slight variations in temperature—all these as well as broad patches of dark and light. When she comes to the grill, she hovers her hand over the pan as if to conjure, but actually to determine whether the heat is evenly distributed. The lard crackles and hisses at her. Its angry spatter stings her palm, but she does not flinch. She walks over to the fisherman and takes the fillets. She drops the fish in a brown bag of salt, pepper, and cornmeal, and shakes it like a tambourine to the random rhythms of the banjo. The fillets jitter when she drops them in the lard.

"This is the claw hammer style," the banjo player explains. "That's what they call it, I reckon on account of your hand's like a claw hammer, sort of pluck stroke, pluck pluck stroke, and such. I never could like the Earl Scruggs way, that Foggy Mountain. And my fingers are too crooked up with the arthritis for all the diddly-fast-diddling on the strings. No sir, it's always been the claw hammer has served me just fine, and it's been good enough to get people up dancing.

"Now that puts me in mind of how Miss Esther, my sweet wife, could one time cut a rug. Music would get up in her, sometimes at church, sometimes when I was playing the square dance, and she started to shaking, trembling like the palsy and look out! She would bust up the floor like nobody's business.

"That's what happens when music gets up in you."

The general consensus was that Miss Esther was a witch. The primary evidence was that her veiled eyes looked in different directions. One always gazed to the left, which is the devil's side, and the other wandered around, aimlessly it would seem, even when she was hard at a task. Some said there was nothing aimless about it. No, that eye watched the spirits, which were plentiful and not all benevolent.

Miss Esther seldom spoke. Those who had heard her reported whispers, barely audible, and a language with words that no one knew.

The banjo player had brought her home with him years ago from his ramblings. She came from somewhere back in the mountains, people said, from a village that was situated exactly where four states connected, like a crossroads. The banjo player had been smitten, as who wouldn't be in the atmosphere of spells and unchecked desire of a crossroads village, an every place and no place all at once.

It had been rumored that the banjo player had dealings with the underworld, because he would play any venue no matter how sin-ridden. But most people wouldn't hold that against him. He was friendly, they loved music, and he would play a wedding or birthday for a plug of tobacco or a hambone. His staunch admirers insisted that Miss Esther wasn't all bad, either, even if she was a witch.

Miss Esther's dancing has been mentioned. That did not help her case among the Primitive Baptists. But those people were also skeptics about speaking in tongues and the Holy Spirit's movements during Pentecostal revivals. One might quibble over the difference between Holy Ghost and demonic possession, but if the same banjo playing engendered both, and each involved ecstatic gyration and unknown languages, only the Lord himself could tell. So let him distinguish. There is plenty to see and feel in this world for anyone who isn't closed up like the coffin that will one day house him.

Miss Esther had been seen walking across the surface of the river at nights. If she were a witch, why not fly? She liked the feel of the water under her feet. Besides, her movement was less a walk than a glide, like a water strider.

The third one, the fisherman, how did he come here? He drifted up one evening on a raft made of tire tubes. He was an enormous man, larger than anyone in the region. He wore his thick black hair in a braid and had a hoop in his nose. There was room, so the banjo player and Miss Esther welcomed him.

"They gave me a place to lay my head. So I keep us in food—gig suckers, trap rabbit, sometimes shoot a wild hog. Ain't nothing more to it than that. Ain't no drama here except in the music. Maybe you shouldn't make out otherwise when you write about us? Just independence and contentment."

Some say the fisherman is Miss Esther's son, a

werewolf, from back before the banjo player brought her to the creekbank. Others say he is her lover, and they step out on Saturday nights when the banjo player is off earning onions with his music.

There are even a few who claim it's both, werewolf son and lover, doing an Oedipal two-step by the light of the moon. The banjo player laughs, "Like he says, only drama around here's in my music. Ain't nothing more to it than that. People look for drama when sometimes it's nothing but happiness. Like what we got here: independence and contentment. That's all you need to write."

Noise and Silence

Hudson Valley Julys are increasingly like the North Carolina summers of my childhood—blistering days, humid nights. But I have avoided installing an air conditioner because the rumble would drown out the insects. An open window on a summer evening reminds me that we live among a host of singing bugs. A continuous buzzing trill is the Carolina Ground Cricket. Three rapid buzzes is the Common True Katydid, but when a forest full of them sings, the sound is a giant's saltshaker. Once my son Sammy and I camped at a site with an ominous name, The Devil's Tombstone. At nine in the evening, the katydid volume was so intense that we could not hear each other speak.

My middle-aged memory is threadbare, so each year I relearn the differences in their songs. A trill with high overtones=Broad-Winged Tree Cricket, a quick chirpy trill=Jumping Bush Cricket. On Sunday evenings there is a conflict, because just as the insects begin to tune up, I like to listen to a radio show of evensong. Once I was listening to Arvo Pärt's choral setting of John 15, "I am the true vine, and my Father is the gardener." An Estonian composer under Soviet rule, Pärt became disillusioned with composition and stopped writing. He studied early music, especially chant from the medieval Christian church, and was drawn back to composition in modal forms. He had an ear for overtones, the resonance of vast spaces, for dissonances that resolved into harmonies. Silence was integral. When I listened with the windows open, the silences were filled with insect song. The most dramatic—the Common Meadow Katydid, which my guide perfectly described as a "lawn sprinkler"—often overwhelmed Pãrt.

Sammy passed through the room. "So are you changing over to bugs now?" he asked, alluding to my long-term obsession with identifying birds. There was Pãrt on the stereo, the live insect chorus, and the recordings from the online guide that I was playing to confirm my identifications. "I'm not being mean," he added earnestly, "but why give a damn about which bug is which?" I said that it's like listening to an orchestra: you recognize the different instruments, right? He shrugged and walked on.

What I didn't say, but thought, was that I shouldn't be

multi-tasking. I'm stretching my attention thin, listening to several things halfway rather than one thing fully. But I need to call these voices by their names, to recognize them in the total soundscape of the moment. Doing so is restorative, not just of my soul but maybe also of the creaturely world we tend to ignore. It's humbling: I have heard these noises my whole life and never thought of the variety and differences. Even the city block is a green world that we cohabit. If we are to have any experience of the true vine, we have to be still and listen to the sounds from its leaves and branches.

Not the devil, but God, or the spirit, or whatever you prefer to call the "something more deeply interfused" that Wordsworth identified near Tintern Abbey, is in the details of the noise. My church is noisy. Not with babies or wiggling children—we would welcome them, but our openness to the addicted and unsheltered discourages families. It's noisy with the side conversations and restlessness of people who don't "do church" but come to ours. Someone gets up to make coffee, because we meet in a community room, and there is a coffeemaker and heavily frosted cake that Miss P., an institution from the church's old days, has baked. The one making coffee asks if he can get something for anyone at his table. "Tea, sweetie, thank you," says an octogenarian in a whisper that doesn't work. A nonwhisper. How else to describe that phenomenon, the valiant attempt at a whisper that is nonetheless more distracting that a normal voice? Something like a fall cricket's chirp. Two or three people arrive late. They are greeted with waves and more chirps. They make coffee and mill around for chairs. Someone drops a guitar. It's important to mention that the pastor is speaking through all of this, and that everyone intends to be respectful and quiet if not silent. All of the shuffling and tinkling, nonwhispering and fumbling reverberates with good intentions. We want to be still. It's just too hard. There is also no call for false politeness. It's like the family room, where everyone stops by on a Sunday afternoon.

Let me not idealize this space. One cannot meditate here, not for more than a minute. One cannot hear a choir singing Pärt. For awe and mystery, other places are superior. In my experience, those are often upper middle class places, populated mostly by people like me, whose years of church or schooling have taught them to occupy a seat quietly and not look bored. You learn this in college if not in church. Faced with a 90-minute lecture on monetary policy after the end of the gold standard, you must learn at least to sit quietly and appear attentive, and at best to become attentive by finding a means to be interested. An indicator of a successful higher education is the ability to get interested in what most people consider boring, because nothing is, in itself, boring. In full disclosure, I have listened with interest to lectures on monetary policy.

Being still and attentive in church is a similarly learned behavior, and it assumes that the purpose demands stillness and attention. While I would defend our noisy church, I am mostly in favor of increasing the silence in every other walk of American life. We talk too much, especially if "talk" extends to our obsessive overuse of social media. Advocating restrictions on social media expression has been equated to censoring free speech. I have heard civil liberties lawyers declare that we should always seek more speech, not less. But in our time, the salient meaning of "more" is quantity irrespective of the speaker or the quality and content of their speech. Social media platforms are markets, not public squares, "more" translates into dollars, and sensational speech sells, even if it has little substance. The noisiest space in the contemporary US is, ironically, the silent phone into which we constantly pour text, image, and symbol. In hindsight, our greatest shortcoming will have been that we blithely contributed so much language with so little substance, and yet that sheer quantity—that "more" that commands defense—costs minds and souls.

We need less speech and better noise. After evensong on Sundays there is a chamber music show that sometimes features "difficult listening." In György Ligeti's "Ramifications," twelve string soloists split into two groups, one tuned slightly higher than the other, each soloist performing simultaneously, without strict meter or conventional harmony. How to describe the sound-scape that this generates? Eerie, chaotic, agitated…sirens, a plane at take off, bees…none of these associations with dissonance can be called incorrect, but neither do they seem sufficient. Listen again with a quiet mind and without the intent to react with words. What takes place in the body, for example? It's possible that "Ramifications" should be experienced, rather than explained. It is noise that requires close listening. Discernment follows from silent attention.

We should be more discriminating in what we choose to respond to, and in the manner of response. Susan Sontag wrote, "To interpret is to impoverish, to deplete the world—in order to set up a shadow world of 'meanings.' It is to turn *the* world into *this* world." Nearly every social media post that isn't a pet photo or self-promotion is an act of interpretation masquerading as fact. Reposted memes, declarations of solidarity in the form of a picture of the exclamation, "This!", expressions of righteous indignation with frowning emojis—we glance, swipe, and categorize, we pronounce the world this way not that, with a thousand up votes, all while we wait in line at Wal-Mart or Whole Foods, or sit at a traffic light, or turn for a break from our endless email. Assuming that all this social media content is "the world" (God forbid), we quickly and with little forethought turn it into "this world," the one that belongs to our tribe or that our tribe abhors. Nothing and no one have really been challenged or bettered. Discourse has been impoverished by further excess—a paradox that defines public speech in the early 21st century "developed" world.

Around twenty years ago, I first heard the neologism, "overshare." It was a time before cellphones and social media, though the messaging shorthand for "too much information," TMI, is a synonym. At the time, a friend and fellow teacher was apologizing. "Sorry, I'm over-sharing," he laughed, embarrassed by the frustrations that he had unwound around us—starting with a recalcitrant student and his insecurity about how he'd handled it, which led to his analysis of why he's so insecure: new teacher, first-generation college graduate, truly believes school is the ticket out of poverty and ignorance, takes it personally when the kids suck their teeth and roll their eyes, would have caught the hand if he'd ever been so disrespectful to an adult in his day, not that he would ever strike a child, absolutely not, but why can't they see that he cares and is trying so hard? Nowadays, his confessions might not register as "oversharing." There was nothing about bodily functions or sexual proclivities. He may have sworn, but there was no one else around—just two colleagues, decompressing after a week of teaching. It was the proper space for expressing frustration. Hyperbole, sentimentality, nostalgia, false equivalences, and heated rhetoric: all of this is for a back porch, evening conversation over beer with a friend. We were out of earshot, the crickets provided white noise, our chatter was impermanent. There was no reason to broadcast it to the world, and there was no means of doing so at the time.

"OK, boomer!" sighs my student, lumping me into my parents' generation to make his generation's two-word counter-argument. In essence, everyone born after 1999 in the US knows better than to take oversharing seriously. There is, in fact, no TMI because more is always better as long as the recipient understands how to filter it, which everyone in their generation does understand. So the argument goes.

We need less speech and more silence. An idea cannot develop in noise. It can begin there, but it needs silence for its consideration, expansion, and refinement. Let us be at a loss for words. When we react quickly, we rarely understand at a depth that warrants our reaction. We just add to the cluttered soundscape. In the Kolita Sutta, one of the early Buddhist scriptures, the venerable Muggallāna recalls being in seclusion when "what is noble silence?" came into his thoughts. He realizes that when monks stop "directed thoughts and evaluations," they enter the second jhāna, a level of contemplation that he describes as, "rapture and pleasure born of concentration, unification of awareness free from directed thought and evaluation—internal assurance." Muggallāna becomes distracted by thinking about this—that is, he becomes absorbed in "directed thought." The Blessed One appears to him and urges him to, "Establish your mind in noble silence. Make your mind unified in noble silence. Concentrate your mind in noble silence." Muggallāna must quiet the urge to interpret his experience. When he does so—when he stops thinking about silence—he attains it and returns to second jhāna.

The Hebrew canon has a related story. The child and future prophet, Samuel, repeatedly hears a voice calling him in the night while he sleeps. Assuming it's the priest, Eli, whom he serves, he runs to Eli's room and declares, "Here am I." The third time this happens, Eli realizes that Samuel is being called by their Lord and directs him next time to answer, "Speak, Lord, for thy servant heareth." In the biblical traditions, God often speaks in the silence and can be heard only by one whose mind is quiet and prepared. The conclusion of the episode of Samuel's calling is an ancient example of not wasting words: "Samuel grew, and the Lord was with him, and did let none of his words fall to the ground." All of the major translations of this passage use the same metaphor. A word "falling to the ground" is not a seed. To grow, a word must land on an ear, or in a mind. The Lord prepares Samuel's listeners by teaching them how to pay attention, much as Samuel had been taught. From the discipline of silence, where listening becomes possible, the prophet learns to speak words worth hearing—or to recall a favorite metaphor of the bible, seeds that will bear fruit.

There is a traditional gospel tune, "Woke Up This Morning," that brings all this together, especially as Mississippi Fred MacDowell sings it. Each verse names an activity three times—"woke up this morning," "walking and talking," "singing and praying." These are interlaced with the refrain, "with my mind stayed on Jesus," and rounded off with three hallelujahs. What makes MacDowell's blues rendering so powerful is that frequently, seemingly at random, he stops singing but keeps playing. I understand this as an expression and a demonstration. He is overcome with feeling and must pause. His pause and the silence manifest the song's fundamental message: when his mind is "stayed on Jesus," he enters a state for which words are insufficient. This is the noble silence of a mind liberated from rumination and analysis. What is meant by "stayed on Jesus"? For the Christian, Jesus represents clarity of vision, commitment, the unity of intent and action without regard for the self. In Buddhist terms, we might say that Jesus transcends the self/nonself duality. I would argue that MacDowell's breathless silence is not necessarily or exclusively about Jesus. Was it for MacDowell, who was a freemason? Perhaps. But the crucial fact is that the mind is "stayed," that it is concentrated, but not directed. All day and night.

When our youngest son, Jacob, interned at a national park in Alaska, he left his kitten with us for the summer. Like a toddler, Jolene rose before sunrise and could not be ignored. First food, then play. She was willing to let me make coffee between, but to sit down required that I at least had a string toy handy for her to attack while I drank and woke up.

In that August, as one final heat wave rolled over us, I would usually turn on the window fans to capture some of the evening cool before it evaporated. But there was a single katydid who, after a full night of chorales, per- sisted with a solo. He seemed inexhaustible, not unlike the kitten, or perhaps more like a Wayne Shorter or Steve Coleman, whose improvisational reserves seem limitless. It's that quality in katydids, crickets, and cicadas which has attracted so many poets. In her "A Spring Cricket Considers the Question of Negritude," Rita Dove's cricket declares that at evening an "ache would bloom inside" and "I knelt down / to scrape myself clean / and didn't care who heard." His song is pure expression. When children collect him and other crickets in a jar to create a "musical lantern," Dove's language invokes a more sinister entrapment. The "shouts and whistles" of the children and the "round up into jars" recall enslavement, and the crickets' songs become a version of minstrelsy. The children are entertained by the music but also, perversely, by the struggle in the jar, where the crickets climb across each other to find the brim. When they do so, they fall back down, and the children clap. But the crickets also learn "where the brink [is]." I've taught this poem many times—once in Palestine, where despite the language and cultural difference, the students were eager to draw an analogy to their own situation. They noticed that Dove first uses "brim," then "brink," to signify the top of the jar, and after turning to a partner to puzzle over the distinction in Arabic, the whole class became animated. Living under occupation, several spoke up with examples of being pushed to the brink—the bottlenecks at checkpoints, the random searches at Damascus Gate, the tear gas canisters lobbed into the courtyard of the university.

The difference between "brim" and "brink" as units of sound is a couple of consonants—a humming on the lips, or a nasal and click—but the weight of the difference wasn't lost on my students. One reason to teach poetry, one reason to study it, is its economy. Whether in an epic or epigram, poets are concerned about the smallest phonemes and morphemes, and they will turn a phrase repeatedly before calling it finished. Where to break a line, where to punctuate the sentence: these are consequential decisions. Dove's enjambment and stanza breaks imitate the cricket's actions, culminating with that final line, "And where the brink was," set off by itself. In class, when we are fully present and concentrating on the poem, we can easily devote 45 minutes to the line breaks and word choice. We stand guilty of "setting up a shadow world of meanings," but the shadows are cast by the form. We hear the poem aloud a few times to get inside it, as in the first step of lectio divina. No word falls to the ground.

In the pause after the reading, the poem's effect begins to register. I ask us to write, briefly, to observe that effect. To appreciate a poem's economy, we produce and exchange a lot of language, much of it informal and evanescent, which is not to say insubstantial or wasted. On the contrary, all this language is in service of listening to the full range of the poem and of learning to communicate with such texture and precision. Most of it is kept private, in a notebook. We are working toward something worth saying in response to a text that wastes neither sounds nor silence. The poem, like the Buddha or the Hebrew prophet, the katydids or Fred MacDowell, teaches us to be at a loss for words.

Let us be at a loss for words.

Acknowledgements

"Looking Up," *Letters Journal* 13 (Summer 2022).

"The Meadow." *The Dewdrop*. October 2021.

"Red-Necked Grebe." *Bracken*. May 2021.

"Creekbank Imaginary (The Cuckoo, Roud 413)." *Flyway: Journal of Writing and the Environment*. Fall/Winter 2020.

"Poor Jack." *Prime Number*. Issue 181 (Fall 2020).

"Addiction." *Toho Journal*. Spring/Summer 2020.

"A Brief History of the Silver Melon Project." *Sierra Nevada Review*. 31 (2020)

"Green Heron: On Dwelling In Possibility." *Raritan*. 32.5 (Winter 2020)

"Hedge." *Tiny Seed Journal*. 13 March 2020

About the Author

Derek Furr grew up in rural North Carolina, taught public school in Virginia, and lives now with his family in the Hudson Valley. He is a literature professor and Dean of Teacher Education at Bard College. He is the author of two previous Fomite books, *Suite For Three Voices* and *Semitones*, as well as critical works about poetry, sound, and performance.

Fomite

Writing a review on social media sites for readers will help the progress of independent publishing. To submit a review, go to the book page on any of the sites and follow the links for reviews. Books from independent presses rely on reader-to-reader communications.

For more information or to order any of our books, visit:
http://www.fomitepress.com/our-books.html

More Odd Birds from Fomite...
Michael Breiner — the way none of this happened
Roger Coleman — The World Was Late
Bill Davis — Cheap Gestures
Clare Dolan — Museum of Everyday Life
J. C. Ellefson — Under the Influence: Shouting Out to Walt
Derek Furr — Semitones
Derek Furr — Suite for Three Voices
Stephen J. Goldberg — Rants Raves & Ricochets
Joel Grossman — Reading Embodied
David Ross Gunn — Cautionary Chronicles
Andrei Guriuanu &Teknari — Portraits of Time
Andrei Guriuanu &Teknari — The Darkest City
Gail Holst-Warhaft — The Fall of Athens
Sam Kerson — Executions and Democracy
Michael Jewell — The Memoirs of a Paper Doll
Daniil Kharms — Connections (translator Roger Lebovitz, artist Delia Robinson)
Roger Lebovitz — A Guide to the Western Slopes and the Outlying Area
Roger Lebovitz — Blessings
Roger Lebovitz — Twenty-two Instructions for Near Survival
Pippo Lionni — Fat Facts of Life
dug Nap — Artsy Fartsy
dug Nap — Friends
Fletcher Oakes — Modern Mandalas
Puppeteers — Sourdough Rising
Delia Bell Robinson — A Shirtwaist Story
Delia Bell Robinson — The Waters Prevail

Fomite